Clara Barton

Founder of the American Red Cross

Illustrated by Frank Giacoia

Clara Barton

Founder of the American Red Cross

by Augusta Stevenson

Aladdin Paperbacks

Aladdin Paperbacks
An imprint of Simon & Schuster
Children's Publishing Division
1230 Avenue of the Americas
New York, NY 10020

First Aladdin Paperbacks edition, 1986
Printed in the United States of America

20   19   18   17   16   15   14   13   12   11
Library of Congress Cataloging-in-Publication Data

Stevenson, Augusta.
  Clara Barton, founder of the American Red Cross.

  Reprint of the ed.: Indianapolis : Bobbs-Merrill,
c1962.
  Published in 1946 under title: Clara Barton,
girl nurse.
  Summary: A biography focusing on the youth of the
nurse who organized the American Red Cross in
Washington, D.C., in 1881.
  1. Barton, Clara, 1821–1912—Juvenile literature.
2. Red Cross—Biography—Juvenile literature.
3. American National Red Cross—Juvenile literature.
4. Nurses—United States—Biography—Juvenile
literature. [1. Barton, Clara, 1821–1912. 2. Nurses.]
I. Giacoia, Frank, ill   II. Title.
HV569.B3S78   1986   361.7'634'0924 [B] [92]   86-10750
ISBN 0-02-041820-5

To Dr. Percy H. Epler
Whose biography of Clara Barton
was authorized by her

Illustrations

Full pages

Numerous smaller illustrations

Contents

★   ★   ★

Books by Augusta Stevenson

Clara Barton

Founder of the American Red Cross

The Captain's Indian Story

"FATHER, PLEASE TELL ME an Indian story," said seven-year-old Clara Barton. It was a cold winter evening—just the time for a story.

"Are you sure you want to hear another?" asked Captain Barton. "You've been listening to them ever since you were four. I should think you'd be tired of them."

Clara shook her head. "Your stories are much more exciting than the fairy stories my sisters are always telling me."

Her father laughed. "Your sisters have never lived with fairies. I've lived with Indians, and many of them were my friends."

"Your friends? I thought you fought them in a war!" exclaimed Clara.

"We didn't fight all the Indian tribes," said the Captain. "I've visited Indian villages, and I've hunted with Indians. The hunters are still my friends, even after all this time."

"Oh! Tell me about some of the Indians."

"Well, I'll tell you a story about one of the Indian wars. It's about something that happened to me and my hat."

"Your soldier's hat?" asked Clara.

"Yes, and this is the way it was. Our troops were on a low ridge. Across a little valley was another low ridge, and that's where the Indians were. For over an hour we had been shooting at each other. Not right along, of course. Just when we saw a head or some feathers."

Clara nodded. She knew that soldiers tried to fight from ridges, if they could find any. Then the enemy was below them.

"When did the Indians shoot?" she asked.

"Whenever they saw one of our hats. We didn't wear any feathers."

Clara laughed. She understood the joke which her father had made.

"Then we had a big surprise," the Captain said.

"Did the Indians surprise you?"

"They certainly did. All at once they stopped shooting and yelling."

"What made them stop?" asked Clara.

"We thought they were out of ammunition."

Clara nodded. She knew what happened when the ammunition gave out. The other side was sure to win the battle. It was good luck for the people with the ammunition.

"We thought we could capture the whole band," the Captain continued. "We began to get our men together. We were scattered out along the ridge behind trees, rocks, stumps or logs—wherever we could find any cover."

The little girl nodded gravely. She knew they had to shoot from behind cover. Indians always fought that way.

"At last our soldiers were ready, and the command was given to advance," the Captain said.

"Did they capture all the Indians?" asked the little girl eagerly.

"Just then we had another surprise," the Captain continued. "We heard warriors yelling in a different part of the forest, off by the river. They had slipped past us, and we knew they would try to escape in canoes."

"Why did they yell? They hadn't reached their canoes, had they?" asked Clara.

"No, but I guess they were sure they were going to," answered the Captain. "Anyway, we went after them. We jumped over logs. We leaped on and off rocks. We ran whenever we reached clear spaces. It was then I had some bad luck. A low branch knocked off my hat.

"It was a good felt hat, and I stopped to get it. I didn't want to lose it because it was the only one I had."

"Why didn't you just get another hat from the army?" asked Clara.

"There wasn't any way to get clothing to us in the wilderness, Clara. We had a hard time getting food," explained the Captain.

"However, if I had known the trouble this hat would cause me, I wouldn't have stopped. Why, I almost lost my life, and it's strange I didn't. Every time I think of it I wonder more and more about my foolishness."

"What happened, Father?" asked Clara.

"I should have known that other warriors would be roving about the forest. I should have gone on with my company."

"What happened next, Father? What did you do?" Clara asked impatiently. She could hardly wait any longer for his answer.

"I looked for my hat, of course. Pretty soon I saw it on a brier bush. This bush was on the other side of the brier patch, so I had to push through the whole field."

"Didn't the little thorns scratch you?"

"They scratched every inch of skin they could find, my dear. But I finally had my hat. I was afraid the thorns had torn the felt. I held up the hat to examine it. Then came my third surprise. Someone shot a bullet through the crown!"

"While you were holding up the hat?"

"Yes, indeed! A warrior thought it was on my head. I dropped to the ground at once, because I wanted him to think he had killed me."

"The warrior didn't find you, did he?"

"I knew he'd look for me and I knew other warriors would be with him. I was afraid that they would surround the brier patch. Then they would have no trouble capturing me. I decided to get out of that trap fast."

"Did you get out, Father?" the child asked.

"I must have, Clara. I wouldn't be here with you tonight if I hadn't." He smiled and patted her head. Then he continued the story.

"You may be sure I didn't show my head again. I began to crawl out of the patch."

"What did you do with your hat?"

"It was on my head, and it saved my face from the briers. Large hats are better than caps at times, and this was one of the times.

"Well, I was careful. I crawled as quietly as I could, but those Indians heard me. Their ears are as sharp as razors, you know."

"Can they cut things with their ears?" asked Clara eagerly.

"Oh, no, it's only a saying," her father replied. "Now, just as I expected, the warriors began to shoot into the patch."

"Then they didn't think you were dead!" Clara exclaimed. "You didn't fool them!"

"They wanted to finish me if I wasn't. Just then I heard the whine of bullets, but not near, thank goodness. They didn't know just where I was, so I was safe for a time. As soon as I was out of the patch and in a clear space, I stood up and ran as fast as I could."

"And you did get away from them, didn't you, Father?" asked Clara expectantly.

"Not yet, Clara. My troubles weren't over by a good deal. Soon I heard the sound of running feet behind me."

"Oh dear! They heard you!"

"I stopped a moment and listened. There was only one person running. He wasn't making any attempt to run quietly, either. He was so sure he would overtake me he didn't have to be careful. To tell the truth, I thought he would myself. I knew I couldn't outrun an Indian warrior. However, if I could reach the river before he did, I'd have a chance to escape."

"Did you do it, Father?"

"I knew a trick I could play on him. I used all the strength I had. I made it to the bank of the river first."

"I'm so glad!" cried Clara.

"There was no time to lose. I had to play my trick at once. I picked up a large stone and I threw it out into the water, but not very far. I wanted to make ripples so he would think that I had dived off the high bank."

Clara laughed. "You fooled him, didn't you?"

"Wait a minute, child. It isn't easy to fool an Indian warrior. All I could do was to hope I had. The bank was covered with trees, bushes, and vines clear down to the river. Although it was a jungle, I got through and hid under a big mass of vines at the bottom."

"Did you have to stay there long?"

"I didn't have to wait long. The Indian came in a few minutes."

"Did he see you?" asked Clara breathlessly.

"I could see him on the bank above me. I was afraid he would hear me breathing."

"My goodness! Did he hear you?"

"He didn't take time to listen. He began to shoot at the ripples right away. After a while he stopped and grunted. Then I knew the shooting was all over."

"Because he grunted?"

"Because he grunted in a certain way, the way Indians grunt when they are pleased. I knew exactly what he was thinking," the Captain said.

"Was it something funny?"

"Well, it hardly seemed funny to me. He was thinking there was now one less white man that he had to fight."

"But it wasn't true, was it?"

"Indeed it wasn't. It didn't take me long to find my company. In a short time I was helping them drive the warriors back from the river."

"Didn't any of them get across the river?"

"We didn't give them any chance to get their canoes. Before we stopped, we drove them away from the forest."

"I wish I had been one of your soldiers."

"I wish you had, Clara. You would have made a good one. You would have warned me when warriors were coming."

"Me tell you? How would I know. They would be wearing moccasins, so they wouldn't make any noise. How would I hear them?"

"You'd hear them. Aren't your little ears as sharp as razors?"

"Ha! Ha!" laughed Clara.

Now it was her bedtime. She said goodnight to her father. Then she climbed the stairs to the big room she shared with her two sisters.

The Christmas Child

LITTLE CLARA BARTON was like the old woman who lived in a shoe and had so many children she didn't know what to do. Instead of having too many children, Clara had too many parents.

Her father and mother were two parents. Her older sisters, Dorothy and Sally, were two more. Her older brothers, Stephen and David, were two more. Two and two and two made six.

Of course her brothers and sisters weren't her real parents. They just seemed like it because they were so much older than she was. They were grown-up young folks when Clara was born Christmas Day, December 25, 1821.

The Christmas child obeyed them, too, just as she obeyed her mother and father.

There was another difference between Clara and the old woman who lived in a shoe. Clara didn't live in a shoe.

She lived in a cottage on a farm. The farm, on top of a long hill, was located about a mile from the town of Oxford, in Massachusetts.

Clara's father, Captain Stephen Barton, owned the farm. The neighbors said he was one of the best farmers in the area. They said he was as good a farmer as he had been a soldier. There was no one any better at either calling, on the hill or in the valley, they claimed.

He raised fine horses too, and he had a large stable for them. There was also good grassland on top of "Long Hill."

He had his younger son, David, to help him on the farm all the time. His older son, Stephen, could help him only on Saturdays and holidays.

Stephen taught at a distant school during the week. He came home only on weekends. Dorothy and Sally were teachers too. Since they taught at nearby schools, they lived at home. Both of them helped their mother with cooking and housework. All of them were devoted to their pretty little sister.

Clara was really little. She was even small for her age. People said she looked like a very pretty china doll with black china hair and black china eyes.

However, her hair wasn't like china. She had two nice braids. Her eyes weren't like a china doll's eyes, either.

Clara's eyes were always shining because she was happy. She had so much love from her family that she couldn't help being happy. Her sisters couldn't do enough for her. They took her to Oxford every Saturday and bought something pretty, such as a new hair ribbon, for her.

Sometimes Dorothy and Sally bought new shoes for Clara's tiny feet or gloves for her little hands. They often bought goods or cloth to make her several new dresses. They spent many hours sewing and embroidering to make each dress as pretty as possible for their little sister.

Her brothers didn't have the time to take her to town, but they taught her to ride and to swim. Stephen played outdoor games with her to make her stronger and help her grow faster. David had taught her to ride with a saddle when she was five. Now he was teaching her to ride bareback. He would lift her to the back of a tame colt and she would grasp its mane. As soon as he had jumped on another colt, they would go over the fields at a gallop.

Clara's mother, Mrs. Sarah Barton, didn't like this riding. She called it "circus riding."

"Colts haven't any sense," she said. "Clara could fall off, and not one of those colts would know enough to stop, as an older horse would."

"David would be there to pick her up," replied the Captain. "He never lets her ride alone."

"I know he doesn't, but she came home dripping wet yesterday. That young colt Beauty threw her at the creek crossing."

"The creek is only two or three inches deep."

"If it had been ten feet it wouldn't have made any difference to that silly colt."

"Don't worry, Sarah. David won't ever let her go near deep water. He won't let her ride under low tree branches, or gallop downhill, either. He's a mighty sensible boy."

"I know he is but—"

"I think it's a good thing she is learning to ride fast and hard," the Captain interrupted at this point. "She might have to escape from danger some time during her life."

"Nonsense! Did I ever have to escape from danger? You know I haven't, and I've ridden horses all my life."

"We never can tell what will happen to Clara," the Captain declared. "Little as she is, I know that she enjoys excitement more than any of our other children ever did. She is the sort of person who will have adventures."

The summer school vacation had begun. Clara's lessons continued, however, with her sisters and with her brother Stephen.

After a week or two, Mother Barton complained about these lessons. "Clara should be learning to cook," she said.

Her older daughters didn't approve of this at all, and they said so.

"She's too young," Dorothy declared. "She's too small, too."

"We help you all the time, Mother," exclaimed Sally. "You don't need Clara."

"That's right, I don't. But she needs to have a change from school lessons. She is old enough to learn the best way to wash berries, slice apples, seed cherries, and shell peas."

"That kind of work wouldn't be hard," agreed Sally. "Perhaps she could do it. It wouldn't take all her time."

28

"She could still have a few lessons," Dorothy added. "We don't want to stop them."

"I'd like to learn to cook," Clara told them. "Just call me when you are ready, Mother."

Whenever Mrs. Barton was ready, however, Clara seemed to be busy. It was time for her spelling lesson with Dorothy or she had promised to read for Sally. The next time Stephen wanted to help her with her arithmetic.

"I haven't had a chance to teach her to boil water," Mrs. Barton complained to Dorothy on a summer afternoon. "You girls have her working at lessons all the time. You must want to show what wonderful teachers you are."

"Maybe so," Dorothy agreed with a laugh.

"Clara doesn't need to study all summer," declared her mother. "She didn't fail in school last winter. She had very good grades."

"She keeps after us every day to hear her do sums, or spell or read," protested Dorothy.

"I know her grades were excellent," said Dorothy. "But we don't like to refuse her when she asks us to help her. Besides, lessons keep her from getting lonesome, Mother. She has no playmates at all. There isn't a child her age anywhere on the hill."

"I have worried about that a good deal, Dorothy, and so has your father. But there is not a thing we can do about it. We can't leave the farm, and the farm can't leave the hill."

"Playmates don't grow on bushes," Dorothy exclaimed seriously.

"Exactly. That's the reason I wanted her to be interested in cooking. She won't be lonely if she is busy. Oh, I know you girls keep her busy, but her mind needs a rest too. She isn't a strong child," Mrs. Barton explained.

"You are right, Mother. I'll tell Stephen and Sally. I promise you there will be no more lessons this whole summer."

"I think that will be better for Clara."

"She can help you in the evenings all winter," Dorothy continued. "You always have plenty of things to do for breakfast."

"Evenings!" exclaimed her mother. "You know well enough what goes on in this house every single evening."

"What goes on?" asked Sally. She and Stephen had just come into the kitchen.

"Your father always tells Clara war stories in the evening. He wouldn't like it if I took her away. That's the only time he has with her."

"No, he wouldn't like it. He'd miss her very much," said Stephen. "He says he's teaching her geography and history with these stories."

"Oh, dear, another teacher!" exclaimed their mother. "Everyone thinks that poor child has to be crammed full of knowledge."

"It's a splendid way to teach geography," said Sally. "It's an easy way to learn it, too."

"Clara is learning the easy way from Father," Stephen declared. "He tells her a story about some battle he was in or some march he made. He shows her the place on the map. If he hasn't a map, he draws one."

"He teaches Clara history the same way," Sally said. "She can tell you all about General William Henry Harrison and Chief Tecumseh. She can tell you why they went to war and where all the big battles were fought."

"Because Father was in them," Dorothy added.

"It's a good idea," said Sally. "I believe I shall try it in my school this year."

"I know I shall," said Dorothy.

"I have already tried it," said Stephen. "I used some of Father's stories. My pupils were delighted, and not one of them failed in history or geography last year."

Mrs. Barton had been listening closely. Her children wondered what she would say.

She had good common sense, and they knew they could take her advice every time. All of them waited for her comment.

"I agree with every word each of you said, but I still say that Clara has too many teachers—five too many. That includes your father."

The teachers laughed and said they were quitting. Their mother could take their pupil.

The next day Clara was in the kitchen seeding cherries. "Ha! Ha!" she laughed when the juice squirted out—even when it got into her eyes.

She liked to count the peas in each pod. She tried to get them all out with one motion. She loved to use the biscuit cutter. She liked to see the fat biscuits come out of the dough.

She never failed to count the eyes in each potato she peeled. She didn't have to ask if each eye would make several new potatoes. She often had helped with the potato planting. She was a farmer's daughter.

"It seems strange that one little potato eye can produce a whole potato plant," Clara said.

"Why no, Clara, it isn't strange," Mrs. Barton replied. "The eyes are potato seeds. When you plant one in the ground, a vine will grow from it. In time, potatoes grow on the vine."

"They have eyes that can be planted," said the little girl. "It just goes around and around, doesn't it?" she asked.

Before long the whole family saw a change in Clara. Dorothy and Sally noticed that her voice was stronger. Stephen said that her eyes were brighter than they had been.

"She's happier," said the Captain.

"She's stronger," declared David. "She rides farther and faster than she used to."

"Aha!" Mother Barton said to herself. "Their words prove I was right." She didn't say anything to her family. All she cared about was to have Clara happy and healthy.

34

Emmaline's Golden Hair

ONE EVENING CLARA and her father had the sitting room to themselves. Mrs. Barton was in the kitchen, making bread. The teachers were studying in their rooms upstairs. David had gone to Oxford with some friends.

It was a stormy night. The wind was blowing hard. Shutters slammed. Tree branches raked on the roof. Scary sounds came down the chimney.

Oo—oo—oo—oo! Oo—oo—oo—oo!

Clara drew her chair closer to her father and took his hand. "It sounds like someone crying. I think Emmaline Moore must have cried like that after the Indians stole her."

"Maybe she did," answered Captain Barton. "Do you want a story tonight?"

"I want to hear the one about Emmaline Moore," she pleaded.

"All right, Emmaline it shall be. Do you remember what state she lived in?"

"There weren't any states out there then. It was Indiana Territory."

"Good. I thought I would catch you on that, but I didn't. What state is it now?"

"Indiana."

"Right. Who had charge of the soldier's fort on the Wabash River in Indiana Territory?"

"General William Henry Harrison."

"Who fought under him?"

"Private Stephen Barton. Later on, you became Captain Stephen Barton."

The Captain laughed. "Ha! Ha! I didn't mean that, Clara. Where did General Harrison's men come from?"

"Virginia and Kentucky. But his army wasn't large enough to fight many Indians. Your company went out to help him, all the way from Massachusetts. You walked, too."

"Do you remember the name of the Indian chief who was urging the braves to fight the white men in the territory?"

"Tecumseh. He was smart, very smart."

"Did General Harrison know what Tecumseh was doing at this time?"

"No, he didn't find out for a long time. He didn't know the day Emmaline was stolen."

"Good! One hundred in geography, and one hundred in history for you tonight, my dear." Clara laughed happily and clapped her hands.

"Oo—oo—oo—oo! Oo—oo—oo—oo!" wailed the wind as it came down the chimney.

This time Clara hardly noticed the sounds because her father was beginning the story. She was lost in the tale he was telling.

The Moore family lived in a log cabin on the Wabash River about a mile from the fort where General Harrison was in charge.

Emmaline was the oldest of the Moore children. She was just twelve, a beautiful girl with blue eyes and golden hair. Two long yellow braids hung down her back.

Late one afternoon Emmaline went out into the forest to bring the cows home. She usually did this, and she wasn't afraid. The Indians were friendly with her family. As she went along the path, she was singing.

She didn't know that angry dark eyes watched her from bushes just ahead. She had not heard that Tecumseh had turned many red men against the white people.

As she was walking by these bushes an Indian brave sprang out and seized her. Emmaline was so frightened that she could hardly breathe.

38

The brave was painted for war. His face was hideous with stripes of black and red.

He took a hunting knife from his belt. When he felt the edge with his fingers, Emmaline was terrified. She was sure he would kill her. She wanted to run, but she couldn't because she was so frightened. She was so weak that she wasn't able even to try to get away.

The brave frowned. He wasn't satisfied with his knife. He took a stone from the pouch fastened to his belt and sharpened his knife.

Then the Indian was ready. He put the stone back in his pouch and lifted his knife. With a single stroke he cut off her long braids.

Emmaline didn't like to lose her braids, but she was glad to be alive. She asked the Indian for her braids. He refused to give them to her and threw them on the ground angrily.

"No like," he said. "Yellow hair bad and ugly. Come, go to village."

He made her walk miles, uphill and down. They went on till they came to an Indian village. He left her with an old squaw, and went away.

The squaw made her put on dirty, worn-out Indian clothes and put her to work. All day long she carried wood from the forest. The squaws had to have wood for campfires and cook fires.

They scolded Emmaline for being slow and for bringing small loads. Sometimes they beat her. They kept her hair cut short. They would not allow her to let it grow. She was their slave, and she cried herself to sleep every night.

She wanted her mother and father. She wanted her little brother and sister. She wondered if she would ever see any of them again. Would her father ever find her?

As Emmaline, with other slaves, worked at the hardest tasks in the village, she thought of the good times she used to have at home. Gradually she gave up hope of being rescued.

One day Emmaline was working at the edge of the forest. She was on her knees, scraping a fresh deer hide. The ugly old squaw guarded her.

She had been scraping this hide since sunrise. It was hard work. Every bit of flesh had to be taken off. If even one little speck of fat was left, the squaw would beat her.

She was very tired. Her right arm ached from scraping. Her back ached from stooping.

Suddenly she threw down the scraper and stood up to rest her aching back.

"I can't stand it!" she cried.

"No stop!" the squaw screamed. "Scrape."

"I can't," Emmaline sobbed. "I'm too tired."

"Want lose all hair on head?"

Emmaline knew what she meant. She had seen an Indian girl with her head shaved just yesterday. The squaw had pointed to the girl who had been bent by a heavy load of wood.

"Not our tribe," the squaw had explained. "She prisoner—no mind—so get head shaved."

Now the squaw drew the hunting knife from her belt and cut off a lock of Emmaline's thick hair. She flung down the hair and asked Emmaline, "Want all off? Want to be like prisoner here this morning?"

"No! No!" the girl cried. "I'll work."

Emmaline knelt and picked up the scraper. She saw her lock of hair on the hide. It had fallen there and stuck on a place that wasn't scraped.

"I'll have a hard time getting that off," she thought. Wearily she started to scrape off the golden hair.

Just then a young brave came running. He drew the squaw to one side and spoke to her quietly. She nodded and grunted while he talked.

"He's afraid I'll understand him," thought the girl. "I couldn't, but I know he's talking about me. The squaw keeps looking at me."

The brave left and the squaw hurried to Emmaline. She seized the girl's arm and yelled at her angrily.

"Get up! Get up! We go wigwam. Hurry!"

The wigwam was located in the prisoners' section, some distance from the village. The squaw made the tired girl run all the way.

She pushed Emmaline into the wigwam so roughly that the girl fell down. The squaw followed her and closed the flap tightly. Then she motioned for Emmaline to be quiet. All at once the child heard her father's voice.

THE SEARCH FOR EMMALINE

Mr. Moore had been looking for Emmaline from the day she disappeared. He found her golden braids where the Indian had thrown them.

He knew then that she had been captured by an Indian. He began to look for his daughter.

Four friends went with him. They had no way of knowing the tribe of the village that the Indian came from, so they went from one place to another. All of the men were settlers who lived near the fort. Each one had his gun, his hunting knife, and his bag of ammunition.

They went to several Indian towns before they found even a clue to where they might find the girl. One day, however, they met a hunter who said he had seen a white girl in an Indian village on Fish Creek. He had tried to talk with her, but the Indians wouldn't allow it.

"How old was that girl?" asked Mr. Moore.

"Oh, twelve or so, I should think."

"Did she have yellow hair?"

"Yes, but it was short."

"What was she doing?"

"Hoeing corn," the hunter said. "An old squaw was guarding her. There were several girls of about the same age working together."

"If she wasn't an Indian, why didn't you investigate into why she was there?" asked one of the settlers.

"I started to the cornfield, but two braves ran after me," said the hunter. "They wouldn't let me go there, and they led me to my horse."

"Will you lead us to the village?" Mr. Moore asked. "I'll pay you whatever you wish. That girl is my daughter. I'm sure of it."

"I'm sorry, sir, but it would be very dangerous for any white man to go there at this time. Chief Tecumseh has just left the village. You know what that means."

"Of course!" exclaimed one of the men. "He is going from one Indian tribe to another all over Ohio, urging the Indians to drive out all white people. That may be why she was taken."

"His speeches have excited the Indians," said another man. "They have begun to attack white settlements in several areas."

46

"Then you know why I advised you to stay away from this Fish Creek village," the hunter said. "It would be dangerous for all of us."

"In spite of the danger I am going there," declared Mr. Moore. "I would take any risk to save my little girl."

His friends said Emmaline was dear to them too, and they would go with him.

"Then I will guide you," the hunter said. "I can't be a coward when you men are so brave."

Very careful plans were made for the journey, for a young girl's life depended on them.

The next day they were in the Fish Creek village. Mr. Moore and his friends had gone into the village boldly. The hunter was to enter it secretly and find Emmaline if he could.

"I'm sure I can find her," he said. "I have a pocket full of trinkets any child would want. I think I can persuade some young Indian to tell me where Emmaline is hidden."

"We'll meet you at the prisoners' quarters," Mr. Moore said. Then he and his friends went to talk with the chief.

Mr. Moore demanded the white girl a brave had recently brought there.

"There is no white girl here," the chief said. "We have only Indian girls in the village."

"General Harrison will come with his army," Mr. Moore said. "He will attack this village if you do not give up the girl."

The chief replied that his braves would never capture the child of any white settler. None of them wanted to have trouble with white men. All of them wanted to be friends and live in peace with the white men.

At first neither Mr. Moore nor his friends believed the chief. After a while, however, they began to think that the hunter had been mistaken. They were convinced that the chief was telling them the truth.

Then something made Mr. Moore suspicious. It may have been the chief's offer to let the white men go through the village. It may have been the way he repeated, "You'll find no white girl here. We want to be friends with the white people."

However, Mr. Moore pretended that he believed the chief and said he had always enjoyed going through an Indian village. He enjoyed looking at the wigwams.

His friends, who knew this was just an excuse to go through the village, nodded, smiled, and agreed. They said they wanted to start as soon as they could.

In the meantime the hunter had discovered the lock of yellow hair sticking to the hide. Then an Indian girl had told him where Emmaline was. She received several trinkets for giving him the information. The hunter quickly tied all their horses near the prisoners' quarters. He held a rope ready as he waited for the others.

When the settlers came the hunter pointed to a certain wigwam.

"She is in there," he said softly.

"In there?" exclaimed Mr. Moore. "How do you know? Are you really sure?" He was so excited that he spoke too loud.

"S-sh!" the hunter warned.

Emmaline wanted to cry out when she heard her father's voice, but the old squaw put a hand over the girl's mouth. While the old woman was preventing the girl from calling, the white men all rushed into the wigwam and seized the child.

"Father! Oh, I'm so glad you've come!" cried the little girl. Then she was in her father's arms. He held her tightly.

The other settlers tied the squaw's hands and feet. They stuffed her mouth with old rags. All the white men hurried to mount their horses. Emmaline rode behind her father. Away they sped from danger to safety and home.

A Scream From the Girls' Room

THE CAPTAIN PUT ANOTHER LOG on the fire. When he turned around, he was surprised to see that Clara was crying softly.

"What's the matter?" he asked quickly.

"It's Emmaline," sobbed Clara. "I feel so sorry for her. I never thought about her hair before. Her hair will grow long again, and she will have two braids, won't she?"

"Of course," said the surprised Captain.

"Then I'm afraid some Indian will cut off her braids again and take her to his village."

Just then Mother Barton came into the room and looked at Clara and then at the Captain.

"She is crying about Emmaline," the Captain explained to his wife.

Sarah, being a sensible woman, didn't pet her little girl. She didn't promise Clara a piece of gingerbread if she would stop crying.

"So that's it!" said Mrs. Barton. "I used to cry over Emmaline Moore myself. We . . . come with me, Clara. The bread is ready. You can grease the pans for me."

Five minutes later the Captain heard Clara's gay laugh. She seemed to have forgotten about the troubles of Emmaline.

"Sarah's a wise one," he said to himself. "She always knows what to do."

That night, long after everyone was asleep, a loud, terrified scream came from the girls' room. It woke everyone in the house. Mrs. Barton put a shawl over her shoulders, lighted a candle, and hurried upstairs. Mr. Barton wrapped himself in a quilt and followed her.

As they reached the top of the stairs, Stephen and David came from their room, each wrapped in a quilt and carrying a candle.

The captain opened the door and the four people entered the room together. Sally and Dorothy were sitting up in bed wide-awake.

"What happened?" asked Sarah. "Who screamed?"

The girls pointed to the trundle bed where the little girl slept. "Clara screamed in her sleep," said Dorothy. "She woke us up."

"She had a nightmare," said Mrs. Barton.

Clara screamed again. Her mother gently shook her until she opened her eyes.

"Mother! Father! save me!" she cried. "Indians cut off my hair! They didn't like it. They said it was too yellow."

"Put your hand on your head," said her father. "Your hair is all there."

"Two braids," David added.

"And both black," said Stephen.

Clara felt her two braids. Then she opened her eyes wide.

"Why, my braids are there," she cried. "But I saw the two Indians, and I heard them talk."

"Did they say they didn't like blondes?" asked Stephen, smiling at her.

"Yes," nodded Clara gravely. "My braids were yellow when the braves held them up. I saw them plain as anything. I saw an Indian take a knife from his belt and cut them off."

"You were dreaming about Emmaline Moore," said her mother.

"Of course!" said the others.

Then Mrs. Barton sent the others back to bed. She sat by Clara and held her hand until the little girl went to sleep. As soon as the child was asleep the mother went thoughtfully down to the sitting room. Captain Barton was already there, and he looked worried and anxious.

"How is she, Sarah?" asked the Captain as his wife came into the room.

"She's asleep now. I hope she won't have any more bad dreams tonight." Sarah sat down by the fire and wrapped her shawl around her.

"Stephen," she said firmly, "it's time for us to have a talk. I think Clara has heard far too many of your Indian stories."

"I've been thinking that myself, but the story of Emmaline never upset her before."

"She's older now, and she understands more what Emmaline suffered," Mrs. Barton said.

"That may be the reason."

"I have noticed for some time that Clara gets upset if she hears about cruelty or suffering," Mrs. Barton went on.

"The other children didn't worry about Emmaline's troubles. I doubt if any of them ever dreamed about her."

"I know they didn't have nightmares about any of the characters in your stories," Sarah said, smiling at him.

"I'll have to find a new way to teach Clara," declared the Captain. "Maybe I'd better stop my storytelling altogether."

"No, your way is all right," said Mrs. Barton. "Just leave out cruelty and suffering."

"I could tell her about the funny things that happened in camp."

"She'd like funny stories just as well as the ones you have been telling her."

They were quiet for a few moments. Then Sarah spoke again.

"Stephen, I'm beginning to think Clara is different from our other children."

"I'm beginning to think so myself, Sarah."

Charming Animals

A WHOLE YEAR had passed. It was summer vacation again. Clara was eight and a half.

The teachers were home, but they had to study for examinations. They didn't have any time to spend with Clara.

"Mother," Dorothy said one day, "I do wish you would let Clara play with dolls. She wouldn't be so lonesome if she had some dolls."

"She isn't lonesome. She has too many pets."

"All little girls want dolls. You let Sally and me play with them."

"I know I did, but I have changed my mind during these last few years."

"Why shouldn't Clara play with dolls?"

"I don't want Clara to love something that is not alive. I'd prefer to have her love animals. I'd like to have her learn their habits and how to take care of them."

"I agree with you, Mother. The animals will return her love, too."

"Indeed they will, Dorothy," said Mrs. Barton. She will find how grateful they are for help and affection. Best of all, she will come to know that they are a part of God's world."

"I don't quite understand——"

"She will find they are very much like human beings. If she has pets constantly around her, she will never allow anyone to mistreat them."

"You always know best, Mother! You are wiser than any of the rest of us will ever be. I'll never ask about dolls again."

"Clara can have all the pets she wants," said Mrs. Barton. "There's room on the farm."

In yet another way Clara was like the old woman who lived in a shoe and had so many children she didn't know what to do.

Her cats and kittens followed her from room to room. Her dog followed her about the yard, and so did a hen, a rooster, a turkey gobbler, and several ducks and geese.

There was a pet calf in one pasture and a pet colt in another. They ran to meet Clara every time she went to see them.

She declared they all talked to her. She said the hen, rooster, duck and turkey called to her to see the bugs they found. They were proud of being smart. She could tell just what they said by the sounds each of them made.

"The colt wants me to watch him run," she told Sally. "He's proud of himself, too."

"What is the calf proud of?"

"I haven't found out yet, but I will."

60

"I can understand why you pet pretty animals, Clara," said Sally, "but I don't see how you can touch that gobbler. He's so fierce-looking that he scares me."

"He likes to be petted," Clara declared. "My little snapping turtle does, too."

"You don't mean to say you pet that snapping turtle!" Sally exclaimed in astonishment.

"Of course I do. It sticks its neck out to be rubbed whenever I come near it."

"It will snap at your fingers some day," Sally warned her. "It won't let go, either. You know that, don't you?"

"Yes, I know," Clara said. "Dave told me that snapping turtles had to be killed sometimes to get rid of them. But mine is different."

"Why do you touch it?" asked Sally.

"I didn't till I had talked to it a number of times. Now I know it won't snap at me."

Sally looked thoughtfully at her gentle little sister.

"I believe you charm animals with your voice, Clara," she said. "They know they can trust you because your voice is so gentle and kind."

"I guess they know I like them," said Clara.

"Because your voice shows it!" exclaimed Sally.

"Come quick, girls! Patch has been hurt badly!" David suddenly called from the barn.

CLARA'S NURSING SKILL

Patch was David's hunting dog. He was a handsome big hound, white with patches of dark brown. His long silky ears were brown. His eyes were large and intelligent.

The whole family loved him. He was almost one of the family. Clara declared he came every day to her to say good morning.

Now he was lying on a pile of hay on the barn floor. Clara sobbed when she saw that the dog was in great pain.

"He was run over by a wagon," David explained. "His paw was mashed. He won't let me touch it."

"Something must be done for his paw quickly," said Sally. "We can't leave him like this."

"Maybe he'll let me work with it," said Clara. "I took care of Stephen's dog when its leg was hurt. Let me try."

"It's her voice," said Sally. "She knows how to charm animals."

"I don't know what it is, but I hope it will work with Patch," said David.

"I'll know what I can do as soon as I talk to Patch for a while," said Clara. She sat down on the hay near the dog, but not too near. She was very quiet. She didn't move or speak.

"If he growls and shows his teeth you must not even try to touch his foot," David warned. Then he sent Sally to the house for hot water, liniment, and bandages. He stood helplessly by the side of the dog, wishing he could help.

Soon Clara began to talk. Her voice was soft, gentle, and sweet.

"Poor Patch, poor Patch!" she said again and again. "I'll take care of you."

She put her hand gently on the sore leg. Then a wonderful thing happened. Patch licked her hand.

"Poor Patch, poor Patch," Clara said. "We all love you and want to make you well."

"It's all right now, Clara," David said softly. "Go ahead. He won't even growl."

Meanwhile Sally had come with the things from the house. She stood by waiting to help.

Clara washed the dog's paw with hot water and put liniment on it. Then she took a clean white bandage and bound it around the crushed paw. As she was working she talked to him quietly. When she had finished he licked her hand again.

"That's a fine job, sister," said David. "I'm proud of you."

The whole family praised her, but her father's words were the best of all.

"You were a good soldier, my dear. You were a brave soldier," he said.

THE LITTLE DOCTOR

It wasn't long till the neighbors were talking about "that wonderful little Clara Barton."

"She has a way with animals," they said. "She knows what to do with them when they are hurt."

Children began to bring their sick pets to her. Susie White brought a sick kitten all the way up the hill. Clara bathed the kitten and washed it every day with warm sassafras tea to get rid of fleas. The kitten was well in no time.

Fannie Curley brought her sick dog up from the valley. She carried the large dog all the way. Clara said its food had been too rich. She fed it bread and milk and cured it in a week.

One morning Andy Curley found his pet ground hog crippled by a dog bite on its leg.

Andy's father wanted to shoot the animal, but the boy couldn't bear that. The pet grew worse and refused food. Andy knew that it could not live long unless something was done quickly.

Fanny suggested taking the pet to see if Clara could make it well, but Andy was afraid that the boys would make fun of him for going to a girl for help. When he realized that his pet was going to die unless it had help, he took Fatty to Clara. By that time he didn't care if the boys did laugh. He told her the ground hog was tame. She needn't be afraid it would bite or scratch.

Mr. Barton said no wild animal was tame when it was suffering. He would help Andy hold it so that Clara could examine it.

However, no one had to hold it. Clara talked to it a little while. After that it didn't move when she treated its leg and bound it. In a surprisingly short time it was well. Andy was amazed at what Clara had been able to do.

Andy told all the boys what Clara had done for his pet. Not one of them even smiled. Instead of teasing him, they said they would take their own sick pets to Clara. Girls could do certain things all right.

One day Captain Barton said that Clara would have been a great help in his camps. Soldiers always had some pets that needed care. There had been lame ducks, quails, rabbits, robins, blackbirds, and dogs. There were sick foxes, chipmunks, weasels and squirrels.

"Why, one soldier had a pet skunk with a bad foot!" he said.

"A skunk!" exclaimed Clara.

Her father nodded. "She was a little beauty. I can see her now. She had soft fur, black as midnight. A broad white stripe ran down the middle of her back, from her head to the tip of her tail. Her blue eyes twinkled with mischief, and she was affectionate and playful."

"But, Father, didn't she ever—? You know—"

"Yes, but she didn't, not once, when she lived with us. She was a very well-behaved animal."

"What became of her?"

"Her foot hadn't healed, so she had to be left with a friendly Indian."

"I wouldn't have left her behind, even if—"

"She never caused any trouble. She knew her friends and treated them as friends."

The Captain and Clara laughed together at the idea of a little lady skunk.

"Don't tell your mother this skunk story," the Captain warned. "She would be afraid you would really take care of one."

"I would," declared the girl.

"No, no, Clara. Your mother—"

"I would if the poor thing was hurt."

Her father looked at her closely. "I believe you would, Clara. You would care for it without thinking about yourself at all."

Moving-Cousins-Leeches

Mrs. Barton had told Dorothy that the family couldn't leave the farm and that the farm could not leave the hill. However, both things happened. The Barton family left the farm, and the farm left the hill.

Now the farm was in the valley at the foot of Long Hill. Captain Barton had bought three hundred acres there. He needed more grassland for his horses and colts. He needed the three big barns on the place.

He didn't need the big farmhouse but since it was there, the family moved into it. The house was three times as large as the cottage.

This house had porches, a balcony, and a big attic that was like a third story. There were fourteen rooms, and seven of them were bedrooms. The attic was one big room, but there were three beds in it. Clara worried about what to do with so many bedrooms. Dorothy, Sally, and Stephen were home only for week ends.

"Wait and see," said her father. "We may have company. We have asked your Aunt Hattie Learned and her children to visit us."

"We want them to stay all summer," Mrs. Barton said. "Then you will have someone to play with, Clara. All four of your cousins are about your age. The two boys are a little older, and the girls are a little younger."

"In case four won't be enough, I have invited Lovett Stimson for the summer, too," the Captain said. "He is a fine boy about your age."

"Is he my cousin, too?" asked Clara.

"No, he is the son of a good friend of mine."

"We don't want you to get lonely in this big house," said her mother.

The next day the company came, all six people. Clara found out how her family could use seven bedrooms. The house was full of people.

The two Learned boys, Sam and Billy, and Lovett Stimson were given the big attic room with the three beds. Sam and Lovett were both thirteen, and Billy was eleven.

The Learned girls, Florence, nine, and Bessie, seven, had a room on the second floor, and their mother's room was next to theirs.

Clara had a room across the hall. No longer did she have a trundle bed. Her room had a high bed and a bureau. By the bed there was a stand with a wax candle in a brass candlestick. She had shelves for her books and a little rocking chair. White ruffled curtains hung at the two windows. There were braided rugs on the floor, and a large china cat held the door open.

The door had to be open, for all the children wanted to look in this pretty room whenever they went by. Often they went inside.

The other bedrooms were for Captain and Mrs. Barton, Sally, Dorothy, Stephen, and David. On week ends all the bedrooms were in use.

On many evenings every chair and stool in the big sitting room was taken by grownups. All the boys and girls would sit on the floor around the fireplace. Although it was summer, the evenings were cool and there was always a small fire.

The lonely-looking dining room was a different place now. There had been one little girl, eating quietly with her parents. Now six children sat around the big table, eating, laughing, joking, and talking.

Clara enjoyed the company so much that sometimes she almost forgot to eat. She had never been so happy in all her life. Five playmates! Just think of it! Five!

The children were seldom home for the dinner at noon. They were out and gone with a big basket of food.

They ate lunch in the woods when they went to get blackberries. They often went to the saw-mill and ate their lunch on the logs. Whenever they went there, they usually stayed all day because they had such a good time.

They took turns riding out and back in the saw carriage. Florence and Bessie were afraid to go, but not Clara Barton. What did she care if the river was far, far below as they rode out over it? She waited for her turn, and she missed no chance for a ride.

When they went exploring for caves, they always took the basket of lunch with them. It was exciting to sit in a half-dark cave to eat. It was even more exciting to hear the echo of their own voices when they called out.

However, they never went far inside the cave. The Captain had told them to stay close to the opening, and they obeyed him.

"Sam, you and Lovett should take a good look inside a cave before any of you enter it," the Captain told them. "There might be a snake or a wild animal in a cave."

Once Lovett did see a furry animal asleep in a cave. He said it looked like a wildcat. The explorers got away from that place quickly.

Whenever they went fishing they took a basket of food. On these expeditions, though, they did not take any meat. They would build a fire and cook and eat the fish they caught.

Clara had more fun that summer than she ever had had before. She wished the visitors would never leave. She climbed trees with the others and swung from high branches. She slid down the haymows, and she played games. She did everything the others did.

She even tried to cross the river on teetering logs. The river which ran through the farm was actually no wider than a creek, but it was deep. Her girl cousins wouldn't even try to go across on the logs. They watched Clara try to follow the boys across. Although she fell in again and again, she was soon back on the logs. Fortunately, David had taught her how to swim.

Finally she was able to cross without falling off the logs. She had learned to keep her balance and did not fall in again.

Captain Barton encouraged all the children to ride his horses and his colts. He let his visitors take the choice of the animals that he considered safe for them and allowed them to ride whenever they wished.

The boys rode bareback, Indian fashion, with their knees up against the horses' necks. They had always ridden that way, but they were surprised to see Clara riding like an Indian.

Clara rode races with them and nearly always beat them. The boys were amazed. They had not realized that she had been riding horses most of her life.

Her father didn't brag about her to his guests, but he certainly bragged to Sarah.

"Clara can do anything they can do, and she can do it better," he said. "She is growing to be a tall, strong girl, and she has a good tan. This summer has been good for her."

"I know she is stronger," declared David. "I saw her pole a raft down the river yesterday."

"The boys thought she couldn't do it, but she did," said the Captain. "She got that raft down quicker and better than any of the others."

"You two aren't bragging, are you?" asked Stephen, winking at the others.

"Oh, no, no indeed!" David said. "I wouldn't do that—not about Clara."

"Oh, no!" laughed Sally and Dorothy.

The river flowed through the pasture and then through the woods. In one place in the woods it spread out and made a shallow pool. The girls always went there to swim because their mothers wouldn't allow them to swim in any other place.

The boys swam at a certain place near the mill where the water was deep. They wouldn't think of going to a shallow pool at their age.

The girls liked their pool in the woods. It was shady and cool. Tall grasses and ferns grew to the edge of the water. There was a carpet of moss they liked to sit on, and there were pretty water plants floating over the pool.

They had only one objection to swimming there, and that was the number of waterworms or leeches in the water. The girls would find one or two of these unpleasant worms on their skins as soon as they had been in the water a short time. They disliked these creatures intensely.

"Leeches don't hurt. You don't know they're on you till you come out and see them," Florence told her mother. "It's always hard to get rid of them, though. Sometimes they're stuck so tight you pull them apart before you get them off."

One afternoon when the girls were swimming in the pool, Dr. Ward came along with a large glass bowl. He called to them. They came out at once and waited to see what he wanted.

He told the girls the pond was the place where he got waterworms and that he would pay them a penny apiece for every one they found for him.

"The leeches mustn't be pulled apart," he said. "I don't want them for fishing bait. I want to put them on a sick patient."

The girls knew that leeches were supposed to cure people. The worm sucked the bad blood out of a sick person until its own body was filled. Then it was taken off, and another hungry leech was put in its place.

"There are two on my arm now, but Clara will take them off," said Bessie. "She's better at getting them off than anyone I know. I always wait for her."

"I do too," said Florence. "She's even better than Mother is."

"Let's see how you get them off, Clara," said the doctor, who had listened to the conversation with interest.

He watched her closely as she took the leeches from Bessie's arm. He was surprised at her skill and speed.

"I never saw anyone do a better job," he commented when Clara had finished. "I wish I had you to take them off my patients."

He told the girls to let him know as soon as they had the bowl half full of leeches and promised to stop for them. By this time the three girls had agreed to provide him with waterworms whenever he needed them.

Florence and Bessie teased Clara all the way home. They called her such names as "Dr. Worm" and "Nurse Leech." They thought the names were very funny, and so did Clara.

She didn't mind teasing. Her sisters had also teased her this summer. They had called her a tomboy, but Clara knew they were only pretending to be shocked. She knew they were really glad to have her climbing trees, walking logs, poling rafts, and sliding down haymows.

The whole family was glad, because Clara was getting stronger, healthier, and prettier.

A Bashful Girl

SEPTEMBER 15, 1831, had come. It was a great day for Clara, a day she had been thinking about all summer.

She had looked forward to this day, but since it was here, she was sorry. She was going away from home on this morning, and she would be away for a whole year. She was only ten years old, but she was going to a boarding school.

Some people called it an academy. Whatever it was called, it was a large school with several teachers. Clara would not come home until the Christmas holidays—three months away. She had never spent even a night away from her family.

The academy was in Massachusetts, but it was a day's journey by stagecoach. Clara had to take the long trip alone. Her mother was needed at home. Her father and David couldn't leave the farm at this time, and the teachers of the family were busy in their schools.

For the first time in her life Clara would not have anyone to depend on. She would have to manage all by herself. No wonder she was suddenly sorry it was September fifteenth.

It was now a quarter to seven in the morning, and the stagecoach was due in fifteen minutes. Clara went to her room for her wraps. David followed to get her small trunk. The rest of the family waited on the front porch.

"She is really too young to leave home," said the Captain doubtfully.

"It has to be this way," his wife said firmly. "Clara failed in the school here. She could not get along at all."

"Mother! How can you say that?" Dorothy exclaimed. "Clara has always received excellent grades. She is two years ahead of most of the children her age!"

"Indeed she is!" said Sally. "She could read when she was three, and she started to school at four. What do you expect of her?"

"I know," said Mrs. Barton. "What you say is true. But something happened this year that we haven't told you about. All of you know how shy Clara has always been with strangers."

The others nodded. They listened closely as Mrs. Barton continued.

"Instead of outgrowing her shyness, she grew worse this past year. Her teacher came here to discuss it with your father and me a number of times. He didn't know what to do with her."

"He said she wouldn't recite half the time," said the Captain. "She would shake her head as if she didn't know the answers."

"He felt sorry for her. He said she stammered and blushed whenever she read aloud," added Mrs. Barton. "He asked us what to do."

"Oh, dear!" cried Sally. "I thought she was a beautiful reader. She didn't stammer and blush when she read for me."

"How did she get along in spelling?" Stephen asked. "She never missed a word when I helped her with her spelling."

"She missed so many words that the other pupils wouldn't choose her when they had a spelling match," answered the Captain.

"The only thing that saved Clara was her written work," said Mrs. Barton. "Every one of her papers was marked 100."

"Well, then she didn't actually fail," argued Dorothy. "She certainly understood the work if she could write everything well."

"I call it failure," replied her mother. "You can't go through life writing everything down."

"Not many people can express what they want to say in writing," Stephen protested.

"You won't get along in the world if you can't tell what you know," Mrs. Barton declared.

"Her teacher advised us to send Clara to this academy," the Captain explained. "He said she would be forced to talk if she was with strangers. He thought being away from home would be good for her."

"She certainly will have to stand up for herself in a boarding school," said Sally. "She's pretty young to hold her own the way I had to. At first the girls walked over me."

"I learned to hold my own there, too," said Dorothy. "The girls will certainly walk right over you if you don't."

"Sh—sh!" warned Stephen. "Here she comes. We mustn't say anything to frighten her. She's been looking forward to this all summer. Perhaps boarding school is just what she needs."

David came downstairs with Clara's small trunk on his shoulders. Clara followed him outside and stood on the porch with the rest of the family. She wore her new red coat and red hat. She was as pretty as a picture. Her dark eyes were shining with excitement.

She was starting on a great adventure. She had a trunk full of new clothes. She was especially proud of the four beautiful new woolen dresses. She didn't know whether she liked the blue, the yellow, the red, or the green one the best. She was sure that no one else would have clothes as pretty as hers.

When it was time for the coach the rest of the family followed David and the trunk to the roadside. All of them tried to look cheerful.

"Don't be afraid of strange girls, Clara," her mother said. "They will be friendly if you give them a chance. I hope you will make many new friends while you are at the academy."

"Don't forget you can read as well as anyone your age," said Dorothy.

"Show them how you can ride if you can find a horse," said David.

"You know the multiplication tables perfectly. Don't be afraid to say them," said Stephen.

"Don't be afraid to wear your new dresses to classes," Sally advised.

The coach with four horses was coming down the road. When it stopped the driver tied the small trunk to the top of the coach. After Clara had been hugged, kissed, and lifted to her seat inside, the driver cracked his whip. The horses started on a run. The little passenger was on her way to her big adventure.

The other passengers smiled at the young girl and tried to talk to her. She barely answered them, though, so they let her alone. There was so much jolting in the carriage that there was not much chance for talking anyway.

The horses galloped over rough roads and even downhill if the road wasn't too steep. The only time they walked was when they went uphill.

The team was changed every two hours, and this pause gave the passengers time to get out of the coach, walk about, and talk. Clara always got out, but she was too shy to walk with any of the other passengers. She kept by herself, and she wouldn't say a word to the others.

At noon the coach stopped at an inn. It was a lovely old stone house with ivy growing all over it. Passengers always ate there.

These travelers invited Clara to have lunch at their table, but she refused. She said she was not hungry, but she was hungry. She had eaten an early breakfast. She had been too excited to eat very much.

Her father had given her enough money for her lunch. The money was in her purse.

Clara thought she just couldn't go into that big dining room to eat. She was bashful and afraid that everyone would watch her, so she decided to walk about while the others ate. After she became tired of walking, she sat in the coach until the other passengers returned.

During the afternoon a passenger offered her an apple, but she was too shy to take it. Then someone offered her a cooky. She was so hungry by that time that she accepted the cooky. She didn't eat it, though. She was afraid that all the people in the coach would watch her eat.

It was dark by the time the coach stopped at the academy. A teacher, Miss Gray, was waiting at the gate for her.

Miss Gray knew how to treat new pupils. Most of them were shy at first, so she did not think Clara was different. She took the little girl to a pretty little room with just one bed.

"After tonight you will sleep in a larger room with three roommates," she explained. "Each of you will have a bed of her own. Our supper is over, so I will send a tray to you here."

After she had told Clara about the rising bell and the breakfast bell, the teacher left. Clara looked around the room.

Presently she hung the red coat and hat in the closet. By that time a good hot supper had been brought to her on a tray. There was no one to watch her, and she ate all the food.

Far away, the Bartons were sitting in front of the fire in the living room. They had talked of Clara during most of the supper hour, and they were still talking about her. They hoped that the other travelers had been nice to her. They hoped Clara had talked to them. They hoped she had had a good lunch at the inn.

Dorothy felt bad because she hadn't told Clara to look at the pictures of George Washington at the inn. She knew Clara, who was always interested in history, would like to see them.

"Don't worry about that," said Sarah. "Clara would be too bashful to look at them. I wonder if she even ate her lunch."

"Clara will be a different person when she has to rely on herself," said Stephen.

"I hope so," said the Captain. "We have all protected Clara more than was good for her. She is so bashful that she is unable even to speak to other people."

All of them shook their heads and hoped that boarding school would help Clara to get over her painful shyness.

That night each one of them said a prayer for their dear, shy little Clara. They asked God to give her the strength to fight her own battles.

The Boarding School

THE NEXT MORNING Clara jumped out of bed the minute she heard the rising bell. She knew she had a half hour to dress.

She couldn't decide which dress to wear. She unlocked her trunk and looked at the four lovely new dresses. Which should it be, the blue, the red, the yellow, or the green?

Finally she decided to wear her old dress, the brown one she had worn for her journey. If she wore one of the new dresses the first day, the girls might think she was trying to show off and they wouldn't like her. She wanted very much to have all of the girls like her.

She looked forward eagerly to meeting her new roommates. It would be wonderful to have three new friends. The four girls would tell one another everything. Whenever her mother sent her a cake, she would divide it with them. Going to boarding school was going to be such fun. Maybe it would be as much fun as that summer with her cousins and Lovett had been.

She was thinking about the good time she was going to have when the breakfast bell rang. She wasn't ready. She had spent too much time trying to decide which dress to wear. Quickly she braided her dark hair and tied it with red ribbons. Then she put on the old brown dress.

When she reached the dining room all the other girls were seated. All of them looked at her, of course. She was new, and she was late.

It was too much for Clara. She became bashful and timid at once. She didn't lift her eyes from her plate unless someone spoke to her.

The girls at her table tried to talk to her. She only answered yes and no, and she spoke so low that no one could hear her.

"The cat has her tongue," one girl whispered to another. Both girls giggled, and Clara knew that they were laughing at her.

At the morning recess the girls wanted her to play games, but she refused. She didn't give a reason. She just shook her head.

When a girl offered her a cooky she refused it. She also refused the apple another girl offered her. She even refused to take a walk with some of the girls that afternoon after school.

The girls she had refused told other girls, and they told other girls. By night every pupil in the academy knew that Clara Barton thought she was too good to play with the other girls. She wouldn't even take a cooky from Edith, nor an apple from Amy. From that time on, all the girls let her alone.

They didn't offer her anything to eat. They didn't ask her to play games or to take walks.

Poor Clara! She didn't know what to do. She was afraid to tell them she was bashful. They would think she was queer. She was embarrassed all day long every day.

When night came it was even worse. Her own roommates snubbed her. At first they had tried to be friendly. They had asked about her father and mother and brothers and sisters. But Clara wouldn't tell them anything. They didn't know her sisters' names, or her brothers' ages. They didn't know the kind of house her family lived in or what sort of work her father did.

Worst of all, she didn't open her trunk. She didn't show them her clothes. They didn't know whether she had any other dresses. She wore the same brown dress all the time. After a little while they stopped trying to be friendly. Clara was soon ignored by all the girls.

Her roommates moved their three beds close together. Clara's bed was off in a corner and it stayed there. She would listen to them laughing and whispering softly until the night bell rang. Then she would cry herself to sleep.

ANSWERING QUESTIONS

Clara didn't know it, but she was making her teachers a lot of trouble. They tried very hard to get her to answer questions in class, but she would not talk. She would just shake her head or mumble so that no one could understand her.

Her teachers realized that she was bashful and they were careful about the questions they asked her. At first they asked her questions that she could answer with yes or no. At the beginning of the second week, however, they thought it was time for her to recite with the other pupils. They got no response from her.

One teacher thought that she didn't talk because she didn't study. Another one thought she wasn't very smart. The third teacher said Clara was just stubborn.

There had been no written work because there was no paper. At that particular time paper was very expensive and hard to get. All classwork had to be oral.

The situation was exactly as wise Mrs. Sarah Barton had expressed it: "If you can't tell what you know, you won't get along in this world."

Clara wasn't getting along. Worse still, she wasn't eating enough. Miss Gray reported this to the principal. She told him also that Clara was becoming too thin and pale.

Mr. Stone was worried. He sent for Clara and asked her what was wrong. Why wasn't she eating her meals? She simply said she wasn't hungry, and she wouldn't explain further. She couldn't tell him she was too unhappy to eat.

She knew he would ask the reason if she did. Then he would find out how the girls were treating her, and she didn't want him to know.

She couldn't blame the girls. That wouldn't be honest. She knew that she herself was the one to blame. She wouldn't even admit that she was homesick. He might blame the girls for that, too, and it certainly wasn't their fault.

She was wrong about this. Had Mr. Stone known, he would have sent her home for a visit. He always let homesick girls go home for a while.

Clara suffered in silence. She often thought she would die if she couldn't see her family.

THE GOLD BRACELET

The Saturday after Mr. Stone talked with Clara was sunny and warm. On this October day Clara Barton sat all alone on a bench in front of the academy. The other girls were in groups.

Some of them sat on benches together, laughing gaily and talking. Others, their arms linked, walked about the grounds. A few just stood and talked together.

A group of seniors was near Clara. They were talking softly, and she didn't hear a word that they said. She didn't know that they were talking about her.

Now Minnie spoke a little too loud and some of the others whispered, "Sh-sh!"

"I don't care if she does hear," declared Minnie. "Look at her over there all alone as usual. She thinks she's too good to go with anyone."

"She hasn't even shown any of her clothes to her roommates," Belle whispered.

"They say she keeps her trunk locked all the time," Kate whispered.

"I'd give anything to see what's in it," said Bessie. "I wonder if she really has any other dress. She's worn the same one every day."

"And Sunday, too," added Carrie.

"I don't see what she is so stuck-up about," Minnie complained. "I wouldn't be stuck-up if I had only one dress."

"It would serve her right if someone made her open her trunk," Carrie whispered.

The others nodded. Then Bessie said she knew a way to get the trunk open. The girls crowded around her.

"I'll pretend I lent her my gold bracelet and I want it back. She'll have to open her trunk to prove she didn't hide it."

"That's splendid!" exclaimed Minnie.

"Sh-sh!" warned the others again.

There was more whispering among them. Then the group walked over to Clara. They didn't sit down beside her. They just stood looking at her without a smile or a word of greeting.

"Clara," Bessie began, "are you ready to give my bracelet back?"

Clara was confused. She had no idea what Bessie was talking about. "W-w-what b-b-bracelet?" she stammered.

"Why, the one I lent you last Saturday."

Clara was bewildered. She didn't feel well, and she could think of nothing to say.

"Don't you remember?" persisted Bessie.

Clara shook her head. She couldn't remember any bracelet.

Bessie turned to the other girls. "You remember, don't you? You were with me, Minnie, and so were you, Belle.

"Yes," nodded Minnie. "I remember."

"So do I," nodded Belle.

Clara was as white as a sheet now, but none of the girls noticed it. She tried to speak again. She couldn't make a sound.

"Maybe you put it in your trunk and forgot it," suggested Carrie.

Clara shook her head.

"You have done something with it," said Kate. "Why don't you let Bessie look in your trunk?"

"Come on!" Bessie called. "We'll all go and look in the trunk."

"Of course!" cried the others.

They had carried their joke too far, and in a moment they knew it.

Clara fell to the ground. She had fainted.

PUNISHMENT

Three frightened girls ran for teachers. Bessie and Kate stayed with Clara and tried to revive her before the teachers came.

"I'll never forgive myself," said Bessie. "I didn't dream she would take it so hard."

"What if she never opens her eyes!"

"I'd want to die myself."

Just then help arrived. Three teachers came running from the building. They knew just what to do, and presently Clara revived.

She was taken to the little room where she had spent her first night at the academy. There she was put to bed. Soon she went to sleep.

Kind Miss Gray stayed with Clara until she was asleep. In the meantime the principal had called the five senior girls to his office to hear from them what had happened.

"It was all my fault," Bessie began. "I was the one who talked the other girls into it."

"Into what?" Mr. Stone asked.

"I thought it would be funny to scare Clara a little. I pretended that I had lent her my gold bracelet, and I asked her to return it."

"Do you mean you asked her to return something you knew she didn't have?"

"Yes, sir," answered Bessie.

"It was my fault, too," confessed Minnie. "I told her I remembered the very day that Bessie had lent it to her."

"I said I remembered it too," Belle admitted. "I didn't dream it would upset her so much. I didn't intend to harm her."

"None of us did," said Kate and Carrie.

Mr. Stone was indignant. His voice was sharp when he turned to Kate and Carrie and inquired what they had said.

"I said she might have put it in her trunk and then forgot it," Carrie replied.

"Then I said Clara ought to let Bessie look in her trunk," Kate answered.

"What happened then?" Mr. Stone asked.

"I told them to come on, and we pretended we were going to her room," said Bessie.

"Did you really mean to open her trunk without her permission?" asked Mr. Stone.

"No! No!" cried the girls.

"You thought you would scare her into opening it. Was that it, Bessie?"

"Yes, sir. But we didn't dream she would ever faint. We only wanted to see what she had in her trunk. We didn't want to hurt her."

"Would you girls have been happy if Clara had opened the trunk and didn't have another dress?"

The girls were silent. All of them looked at the floor. The joke no longer seemed funny to any of them.

"Tell them, Miss Gray," said the principal.

"She has four of the prettiest wool dresses I ever saw," said Miss Gray. "They are all new, and very stylish. But she has been afraid that you would look at her if she wore them."

"Look at her!" exclaimed the girls.

"She feared you would look at her, and she was so shy she couldn't bear the thought of it."

"Oh!" cried some. "The idea!" cried others. All of them were astounded.

"Girls," said Mr. Stone severely, "you accused Clara of stealing."

"No! No! We didn't mean that! We knew she did not steal anything," cried the girls. "We just wanted to have a little fun and to see what she had in her trunk." They all talked at once. Now they were really frightened.

110

"It's a terrible thing to accuse anyone of a crime," Mr. Stone said sternly. "Clara's father could make plenty of trouble for all of you, and I wouldn't blame him if he did."

By this time the girls were sobbing, but Mr. Stone wasn't through with them.

"Each one of you must apologize to Clara," he told them. "Go to her room now and enter one by one. Miss Gray will be with her.

"Then you will go to your own rooms and remain there all day today and Sunday. All of you have single rooms since you are seniors, but you will not be allowed to have other girls visit you for these two days. Nor can you visit each other. Your food will be brought to you.

"I hope you will spend the entire time thinking of the cruel joke you tried to play on a shy, bashful little girl."

The girls left the office and went one by one to see Clara. Then they went to their rooms.

Three days later Stephen and David came to get Clara. Mr. Stone had written to tell Mr. Barton that Clara wasn't well and ought to be at home. He told her brothers about the bracelet incident while she was getting ready.

"A boarding school is not the right place for Clara," said Stephen.

"Not until she learns to be at ease with other people and to be friendly," Mr. Stone replied.

Clara's Surprise

THE FAMILY DIDN'T TELL Clara, but all of them were disappointed when she left the academy in such a short time. They wondered if she would ever get over her shyness. They began to feel afraid her life would be ruined by it.

At this time, however, they were greatly concerned about her health. They felt that the one thing that mattered at the moment was that she should be well again. School and studies could wait. It made them all sad to see Clara so thin and pale. They hoped she would soon be the gay, bright-eyed little girl she had been before she had left for the academy.

Her sisters were afraid she would be lonely on the farm. The valley children were in school. Clara's best friend, Susie White, could come to see her on Saturdays now and then. Susie had to do a great deal of work at home, though.

In a week or so Clara was busy herself. Her wise mother saw to this. She asked Clara to dry dishes and set the table. She allowed the child to peel potatoes and apples, stir the batter for corn bread, roll out piecrust, and do dozens of other things.

Mrs. Barton gave her outside work also. She let Clara feed the chickens, gather eggs, bring in kindling, and do errands.

Before long Clara was eating more. Her color was better, and she was stronger.

One afternoon she coaxed her father to let her milk a cow. Soon she was milking every day, and she liked it. Before long she could milk a cow almost as skillfully as her brothers could.

David took her coasting when the weather was cold. One mild day he took her horseback riding. He was pleased when she was strong enough to drag a sled up the hill and to mount a horse without his help.

"I would be afraid to wrestle with you, Clara," he said one day. "I believe you would throw me."

Clara laughed. She knew he was teasing her, but she was pleased just the same.

THE ACCIDENT

One Saturday morning in November something unusual was going on at the Barton farm. The barnyard was filled with men, all neighbors. They were good neighbors, too, for they had come to help raise a new barn. This meant they would raise the frame from the foundation to the roof. They were glad to help. Mr. Barton and his two sons had helped them with barn raisings.

Several men were needed to lift and place the heavy posts and rafters. The logs for the foundation were heavy also. Many hands speeded the work. By noon the foundation was made and the center and corner posts were in place. A few of the rafters had been raised and nailed down.

Mrs. Barton had a big dinner for these neighbors. Dorothy and Sally filled all the plates with fried chicken, baked beans, cabbage, mashed potatoes, and hot biscuits.

Clara poured the coffee and milk. After that she helped to pass white and chocolate cake and three kinds of pie.

After dinner the workers rested. During this time they talked, laughed, and joked. Everyone always had a good time at a barn raising.

The younger men stayed in the barnyard to wait for the second table. Just for fun, one of them dared David to swing on the rafters. All of his friends thought he could do it.

David, who was an athlete, took the dare. He was always getting prizes for games of strength. He began to climb a corner post. He went higher and higher. He reached a rafter.

A board had been left there when the rafters were being placed. David stepped on it when he reached up to swing.

It happened without warning. The board fell, and David fell with it. His head struck a heavy timber. He lay there without moving. Everyone feared he was dead. However, he was breathing when they reached him. They lifted him gently and carried him to the house.

Dr. Ward came. After half an hour he was still in David's room. Mr. and Mrs. Barton were also there. The door was closed.

Stephen, Sally, Dorothy, and Clara waited with the neighbors downstairs. All faces were grave. People were silent, or they spoke in whispers. Clara was weeping softly.

Sally put an arm around her little sister, and Dorothy held the child's hand. Everyone who was there waited anxiously for Dr. Ward to come out of David's room.

A DIFFERENT GIRL

It seemed hours before Dr. Ward came down the stairs. He said that David would live. The boy had no broken bones. He did have a fever, but that could be broken in a few days.

They all knew what the doctor would do for a fever. No one was surprised when he asked someone to get the jar of leeches from his saddle-bag and bring it to David's room.

They were surprised by what Clara did. First she called to the doctor to wait, and she pushed through the crowd to the stairway. Her timidity and bashfulness were gone. Even her voice was strong and clear.

118

"I know how to handle leeches, doctor, and I want to help you," she said. "You can't come to see David every day."

The people who heard Clara speak couldn't believe their ears. All of them knew she was shy and timid. She seemed to change as they looked at her. She wasn't the same girl. She didn't blush or stammer or choke on her words.

The doctor was just as astonished as the other people. He knew all about Clara's bashfulness. He had heard the story about the bracelet. For a moment he couldn't answer her.

When he didn't speak Clara thought he was going to refuse her. She began to insist. "I know how to take off leeches, Doctor. You said I did. You saw me take them off my cousin that day at the pool. You said I did it better than anyone else. Don't you remember?"

"Of course, of course I remember. You did get them off nicely," said the doctor.

Clara didn't give him time to ask himself any more questions. "Doctor," she pleaded, "you will let me, won't you? Please say you will!"

"But . . . but . . . I . . . —" The good doctor didn't know what to say. Did this child know what she was talking about?

Then the doctor looked into Clara's eyes and made up his mind. She knew what she was doing. She wasn't out of her head from fright.

"Well, Clara," he said, "I don't see why you shouldn't. We'll talk to your mother and father. Come along with me."

Clara followed him up the stairs and into the sickroom. The door closed behind them.

Dorothy and Sally looked at each other too astonished to speak. They couldn't believe they had been hearing their little sister, who usually was afraid of the sound of her own voice.

The neighbors talked about Clara as they went back to their work.

"My little girl wouldn't touch a leech," said one of them.

"Neither would mine," said another.

"I don't like to handle the slimy things myself," said a third neighbor.

"Nor I! Nor I!" cried others.

Later on Mrs. Barton came down to the sitting room. She said that she and their father had consented to let Clara help with the leeches.

Neither the girls nor Stephen approved of this decision. They said Clara was too young to do such work. She wasn't quite eleven yet.

"We were afraid to refuse," Mrs. Barton said.

"Afraid!" exclaimed the others.

"She begged us so hard and she was so terribly in earnest we were afraid she might get sick too if we refused to let her nurse David."

"Wasn't she just excited?" Sally asked.

"No, it wasn't excitement at all. A feeling came from her heart and overpowered her."

122

"Maybe this is the answer to our prayers for her," said Dorothy.

"She wanted so much to help David that she forgot herself completely," said Mrs. Barton.

"We prayed she would get the strength to fight battles," said Dorothy.

"Ah, but that was her own battles!" exclaimed Sally. "Not other people's battles."

"The strength was given her to fight battles for others," their mother said. "That is what has changed her."

"Nurse Leech" and "Dr. Worm"

MORE THAN A MONTH had passed. When Clara had her eleventh birthday on Christmas Day there was no party. There was not even a Christmas tree, for David was still ill with a fever.

The whole family helped to take care of him, but Clara was his "leech nurse." He wouldn't let anyone else put the leeches on or take them off. He said the other people hurt him.

Clara was glad he wanted her. Her fingers became more and more skillful and her touch more and more gentle as she gained experience. She was devoted to her sick brother. She seemed to know what to do for him.

A dozen times a day she put cold cloths on his hot forehead. She bathed his face and hands with cold water when he was burning with fever.

Sometimes she read to him when he was quiet. He said the sound of her voice made him feel better. One day he smiled and said he was just like Patch. Clara had charmed both of them with her voice. She sat by his bed quietly when he took naps and soothed him when he was restless.

She wouldn't leave the house at first, but her mother soon put an end to that.

"You must get some fresh air and exercise," she said. "You will have to spend at least two hours outdoors every day."

"But David might ask for me."

"The rest of us will take care of him," said her mother firmly. "You can see to the leeches before you go out."

"He wants me with him all the time, Mother. He rests better when I am with him."

"I know he likes you to be near him. But you will break down yourself, my dear. Then I will have two patients in the house. Your father and I have agreed that you must go out."

After that the neighbors saw Clara Barton riding or walking every day. "There goes the little nurse," they told their children.

The old neighbors on the hilltop saw her passing by also. "There goes the little nurse," they said to their children.

Up above and down below children ran to doors and windows to see Clara Barton. All of them wanted to see the little girl nurse.

A year later, when Clara was past twelve, her brother was still ill, and she still nursed him. She still put on the leeches and took them off. She was the only one who could do this without hurting him. She continued to read to him and to put cold cloths on his aching head. She sat by him when he took naps.

Her parents saw to it that she took exercise in the open every day. If the weather was fit she would ride, for she now had a fine horse of her own. Her father had given it to her for a birthday-Christmas present when she was twelve. It was a beautiful horse with slender legs and ankles. It was nervous and frisky, but Clara wasn't afraid.

She understood horses and knew how to manage them without a whip. She rode fast, too. She always beat her sisters when they raced.

Stephen said she sat in her saddle as if she was in a rocking chair.

"It's just as comfortable," Clara declared.

"I wish I could say that," laughed Sally.

"I wish I could, too," laughed Dorothy.

"There's no use talking, girls," said Stephen. "Clara is the best horsewoman."

Not one of the Bartons disagreed. All of them were proud of Clara's horsemanship.

Another whole year passed. David was still ill. Nurse Clara, who was now thirteen, still saw to the leeches. Dr. Ward still called every week.

Everyone was discouraged about David's health. They feared he would never get well.

Just at this time the doctor heard of a place where sick people were cured by steam baths. He advised taking David there. In a short time the young man was better. When he came home he was well. The whole family rejoiced.

Then the three teachers took charge of Clara. They said she should enter high school and that they would get her ready. She would just have to study hard to make up for the two years she had lost while she was nursing David.

Could she do it? Would she be able to pass an entrance examination to Oxford High School? The teachers said she could. Susie White was sure Clara couldn't pass after being out of school for such a long time.

Susie didn't know much about the three Barton teachers. Neither did she know what a good little student Clara was. She had forgotten that Clara always stuck to a thing till she conquered it. It didn't matter whether it was a new game or a new problem in arithmetic, Clara never gave up. She kept on trying.

Two Clara Bartons

CLARA PASSED the entrance examinations for Oxford High School with good grades. For a time she was happy about it. Then she began to seem upset. She couldn't eat. She jumped when anyone spoke to her suddenly. She acted as if she were afraid of something.

The night before school opened Clara went to bed early. Mrs. Barton followed her daughter upstairs and sat down on the girl's bed.

"What is troubling you, my dear child?" she asked "Tell me everything."

Clara confessed that she was afraid to go to school. She wouldn't know how to act.

When Clara went on to say that she was afraid the other pupils would laugh at her, Mrs. Barton was discouraged. Where was the brave girl who had nursed her brother? Where was that wonderful girl who hadn't been afraid to do anything that would help David?

She had been willing to give up school, fun, and parties. She had hardly thought of herself in two years. She had been levelheaded, calm, and thoughtful. It seemed impossible she would ever be shy and timid again.

But here she was—the bashful, fearful Clara again. The brave Clara had disappeared. "She is even worse than she was," Mrs. Barton thought. "It frightens me. I don't know what to do, and her father wouldn't know either."

Suddenly she had an idea! She might be able to scare the timid Clara so badly that the brave Clara would come back. She would tell the secret the family had kept from Clara.

They had feared it would make her ill if she knew that David had threatened to leave home on her account. He had said he couldn't bear for her to be so timid and afraid. He believed it was his fault, and he grieved over it.

"I kept that child in a sickroom for over two years," David told his parents. "I begged her to stay with me when she should have been going to school and having fun with young folks."

Clara hadn't grown much, either, and he worried about that. She wasn't an inch taller than she had been when she was eleven. He said this was his fault too. He had ruined her health by being selfish.

His parents, sisters, and brothers had tried to reason with him. They told him it wasn't his fault. Clara had been determined to take care of him. But he wouldn't listen to them. Every day they worried for fear he would leave, and he still was not very strong.

All this flashed through Mrs. Barton's mind. She spoke sharply to her daughter.

"Clara, you will drive David away from home if you refuse to go to school tomorrow."

"Mother!"

Mrs. Barton told Clara the truth. She didn't smooth things over, either. Clara was sobbing long before her mother had finished. Even when Mrs. Barton stood up to go she said things that hurt. She hoped to help Clara.

"If your brother leaves it will be your fault, my dear child. If you don't enter high school I fear for David—we all do." Then she kissed the sobbing girl and left the room.

The scare worked. The next morning Clara came down to breakfast ready for school. She wore a yellow wool dress, her prettiest one, and she had tied her braids with a yellow ribbon. Her father said she looked like a yellow canary. David's face lighted up when he saw her.

She didn't say one word about dreading school. She was a changed girl. She was now the Clara Barton who had pushed her way through the crowd to talk to Dr. Ward.

The family understood. She had forgotten herself. Again she was thinking only of her brother. They knew she would be all right.

ONE OF THE CROWD

The high school in Oxford was about a mile and a half from the Barton farm. Clara rode horseback every morning, but she didn't ride all the way. She left Star at the White's farm, and she and Susie walked to school together.

There were so many things to talk about. There were lessons, games, Faith Temple's new dress, Emma Lane's party, the spelling match last Friday, the number of pickles Mary Brown ate every noon, and a dozen other things.

Clara was interested in everything and she was a part of everything that went on. She didn't sit on a bench alone here. She went to school parties and picnics. She gave a class party at her home. It was fun to be one of the crowd.

It was wonderful to have her friends tell her secrets, too. Faith told her what she was going to give her mother for Christmas. Emma mentioned the new coat her sister wanted to buy. Hope said she was getting up a surprise party for Cynthia, Clara's cousin, and made Clara promise not to let anyone else know for a while. Clara was a good friend and kept her promise.

Samuel Temple showed her a present he had made for his sister Faith for her birthday. It was a tiny basket he had cut from a peach seed.

Hope's brother, John, told Clara the reason he couldn't enter the skating match the week before. He had broken his old skates. His father could not afford to buy him a new pair.

John told Clara he wouldn't have let any other person but her know for anything in the world. Wild horses couldn't have dragged the secret out of Clara Barton. She knew exactly how John felt about telling anything against his father. She felt the same way about her father.

Sometimes she thought of the secrets whispered from those three little beds at the academy. She had been out of everything because she was the other Clara. She hoped and prayed this bashful, unhappy girl would never come back.

There were times, though, when she knew that the other Clara was close by. She would begin to stammer and choke in class. She would miss words in oral spelling. She missed words that she was sure she knew.

The same thing happened when it was her turn to read aloud. She would mispronounce certain words. She knew the right way to say them, but she would say them the wrong way.

No one laughed at her now. The boys and girls didn't even smile. They pretended they hadn't noticed. They all knew about Clara's shyness, and they knew how she was fighting it because of David. They wouldn't have laughed at her for anything in the world.

Her parents saw the fight she was making, too, and they were delighted. So were her sisters and brothers.

No one was more pleased than David. "She'll make it!" he said over and over. "I know she will make it."

Smallpox!

ONE MORNING, on the way to school, Susie told Clara a secret. She said she felt awfully bad and she hadn't eaten a bite of breakfast. Her mother hadn't wanted her to go to school, but she was afraid she wouldn't pass if she stayed out.

Of course she wouldn't tell her teacher. The teacher always sent home pupils who were sick. Clara mustn't tell anyone.

Clara didn't answer. She looked at Susie's too-bright eyes and flushed face. No one knew fever signs better than Clara. She had lived with and helped to care for a fever patient for two years. She knew the danger as well as a doctor.

Clara immediately told the teacher that Susie was sick. Susie was sent home, and Clara went with her. Clara had intended to go right back to school. However, Mrs. White had to go for Dr. Ward, and she asked Clara to stay with Susie until she returned.

When the doctor came he had just one word to say—"Smallpox!"

The White home was quarantined. The family was not allowed to leave the farm. Clara Barton was not allowed to leave either. The doctor said she had been exposed to the disease and could give it to other people.

David brought clothing to her, but he placed the bundle outside the gate and called her from the road. She talked to him from the porch, but she didn't go for the bundle while he was there.

"Mother said you must not eat fat meat," David called. "Don't eat anything that is fried."

"I know that," Clara called back.

"She said to let butter and cream alone, and pie, cake and preserves, too."

"I know that, too. Dr. Ward told us."

"Be sure you don't catch cold! You'll find a big shawl in the bundle."

"I'm much obliged."

"We all hope you won't catch smallpox."

"I hope I won't myself."

"Well, good-by Clara!"

"Good-by, David!"

After David left, Clara went for the bundle. She sat with Susie whenever Mrs. White was busy. She gave her friend medicine at the right time. She never forgot it.

Suddenly Susie grew worse. Her fever went up. Dr. Ward was called. Clara could tell by looking at him that he was anxious about Susie.

When he found out that Susie's younger brother had given her three large pieces of cake, he was even more anxious.

Clara had not forgotten her mother's warning about letting rich food alone.

"Mother was right," she thought. "This proves it. I must always remember."

Mrs. White was grateful for all the help Clara gave her in taking care of Susie. Clara seemed to know how to make her friend comfortable. She could soothe her when no one else could.

"That child is a natural-born nurse," said Mrs. White. "I don't know how I'd have managed without her. She's been a wonderful help."

When Susie grew better, Clara went out every day for a walk, but she didn't leave the farm. She followed cow paths through the woods and by the creek.

Whenever she saw a pretty pebble or flower she took it to Susie, and the sick child loved her for bringing them. Sometimes Clara saw children playing by the brook. Then she turned back. She never disobeyed Dr. Ward's orders.

Susie was almost well when Clara began to feel bad. Mrs. White sent for Dr. Ward. When he got there, he had just one word to say about Clara. "Smallpox!"

The Barton home was quarantined, for Clara was brought there. She was not seriously ill, and Mrs. Barton was a good nurse. Clara recovered in a short time.

By this time the disease had spread throughout the neighborhood. One house after another had been quarantined. Schools and churches had been closed to check the disease. Dr. Ward was busy day and night.

CLARA HAS A PATIENT

Those who recovered from smallpox couldn't get it again. When Clara's young cousin Cynthia became ill with the disease, her mother went after Clara at once.

"I know you can't have it again," said Aunt Bell. "Cynthia wants you with her. She thinks you can cure her."

"I'm not Dr. Ward," protested Clara.

"She thinks you tell him what to do."

Clara laughed. Then she became serious. "I'd like to nurse Cynthia," she said.

"I'm so glad," exclaimed Aunt Bell. "I'm sure you girls will get along. You're about the same age, and you've always loved each other."

The young nurse did get along with her younger patient. She wasn't very sick. Clara did not have much to do.

Her hardest job was keeping the two older boys out of the sickroom. William was eighteen and Henry sixteen. They were so healthy they thought they couldn't catch the disease.

They hadn't caught smallpox when their mother and father had it, and they wouldn't get it now. They said Dr. Ward was an old fogy.

He didn't know everything—not by a good deal, and they weren't going to obey his rules. One morning when no one was about, they slipped into Cynthia's room. They had been there for a half hour when Clara came back.

She told their father, and he punished them. Then they called Clara a tattletale. They did not say it to her face, but they said it so that she was sure to hear them. If they thought they could scare Nurse Barton from doing her duty, they had something to learn.

They became more and more impatient under the quarantine. They teased their father to allow them to go to shooting matches and ball games. They said they wouldn't get off their horses but would watch from a distance.

Their father refused to let them go, and they pouted and sulked.

"Why don't you act like your cousin Clara?" he asked. "She isn't complaining."

"She believes all those rules of Dr. Ward's," said Henry. "We think they are silly."

"Silly or not, you must obey them. The doctor is doing his best to stop the spread of this disease. We must all help, every one of us."

One evening just about dark, Clara went to the stable to see about her horse. She had no special reason. Star was all right. The boys took good care of her. All of a sudden, though, Clara felt she must have a look at Star. She slipped out of the house.

She was surprised to find the stable door open. She knew her uncle always closed it after he had finished the chores.

She stepped inside the stable. She heard the boys talking. They were saddling their horses and getting ready for a ride.

Clara thought nothing of this. They wouldn't be breaking quarantine if they stayed away from other people

147

They hadn't heard Clara, and she didn't speak to them. They would be sure to think she was spying on them. She waited quietly, hidden in the dark shadows.

Suddenly she heard them say something that astonished her. They said they would have to ride fast to get to the dance, for Newberry was five miles away. With this they were gone.

Clara was horrified. They were breaking quarantine! This was against the law. Everyone at the dance might get smallpox through these boys. Many people might die.

They were carriers! They must be stopped.

CLARA'S PLAN

Clara's uncle had gone to bed. "By the time I wake him, the boys will have a good start," she thought. "By the time he has dressed and saddled a horse, they will be in Newberry."

She must go herself. She had never gone any place alone at night, but there was no time to think of being afraid. People had to be saved. The very thought made her brave.

It was the other Clara who quickly saddled Star and galloped away in the dark night.

She didn't follow her cousins. She knew she couldn't stop them. The sheriff would have to do that. Her only hope was to get to Newberry first. She took a short cut through the woods.

Star could gallop much faster than the boys' horses. She was much faster than most horses, and she proved it that night. In thirty minutes she had covered the five miles.

Clara Barton was in the sheriff's office ten minutes later. A few words were enough for the sheriff. He knew the danger.

In a few moments two deputies went galloping out to meet the boys. The sheriff had ordered them to arrest and lock up the boys.

After Clara had rested he took her back to her uncle's. He wouldn't allow her to go alone.

"You are a brave girl," he said. "You are the bravest girl I ever knew. I can tell you that the people of Newberry will be mighty thankful to you for what you have done."

William and Henry were stopped before they got to the town and taken to jail. When they came home a week later, they had changed. No longer did they think Dr. Ward was an old fogy. They were more than willing to obey the quarantine rules without complaining.

Later on both boys had a serious case of smallpox. They wanted Clara to be their nurse, but Clara couldn't leave home. Her sisters had smallpox by this time, and she helped her mother nurse them.

The disease gradually died out. When there was no longer any danger, schools were opened and business went on as before.

People could visit again and go from town to town as they wished.

Then one Saturday the people of Newberry sent a present to Clara Barton. They wanted to show their gratitude to her. The sheriff brought it and presented it with a nice speech.

It was a beautiful leather saddle made just the right size for the little nurse.

The New Teacher

A FEW MILES from the Barton farm was a little settlement called Texas Village. The settlers were farmers and good people—that is, most of them were. A few of them were rough—mostly older boys.

There was a one-room schoolhouse in the settlement, but it was closed half the time. One teacher after another had been driven away from the school by these rough boys. The teacher who had been there last had found her desk burning one morning. She had left at once.

Now there was a new teacher, and this was her first day. She knew it might be her last day.

She knew it the minute she looked at those big bullies who had come in together. They sat on a long bench right in front of the platform. They nudged one another and grinned. It would be easy to get rid of this one. She was only a girl! She wasn't any older than some of them!

She was small and slender, too. Of course she was weak. They could tell by her looks. And if there was anything they despised more than weakness, they didn't know what it was.

The new teacher told them her name—Barton. Miss Clara Barton.

She didn't tell them she was only fifteen. She hoped they would think she was older. Nor did she explain that this was her first school. She didn't want them to know how green she was.

Her folks didn't want her to take this school. They had heard about the other teachers. Clara wanted to try it anyway. She thought she could control the rowdies by being kind to them.

She had been telling David her plans this morning. The two of them were in the barnyard, putting Clara's books and school things in the spring wagon. David would drive her to school today, but after this she would ride horseback.

"You can't control those rowdies by kindness," David had declared. "They will laugh at you. The only thing they understand is strength."

"Well, I've got it," laughed Clara.

"Indeed you have! Show 'em your muscles. Get up a wrestling match and throw the whole bunch. You can do it. You can throw me, and I'm a far better athlete than any of them. Show them how strong you are before they start anything."

"I am so thankful that you have trained me so patiently, David. Two years ago I couldn't lift a pail of milk. Now I can lift that cider keg."

She lifted the heavy keg without any trouble and set it in the wagon.

154

"You are the strongest girl in Massachusetts. I am proud of you."

David had been working with Clara ever since he had come home from the steam baths. He was determined to build up her strength. He said he owed it to her.

He had taught her to run, jump, lift, and wrestle. Clara was a willing pupil. She didn't want to be puny and weak. Her strength didn't grow all at once. It came little by little, just a little more each day.

The athlete had the right to be proud of her. She was an athlete herself, and a good one.

Today, however, when she stood before her pupils, she was sorry she had not followed the advice of her family. She didn't like the looks of the boys on the front bench. She would have trouble with them before the day was over.

She soon saw that she was mistaken. The trouble began at once.

When she asked their names they mumbled something she couldn't understand. Then the others shouted with laughter.

They shuffled their feet. They coughed often and loud. They talked out loud while she had a class of younger pupils.

When she called on them to recite, they looked out of the window and pretended they didn't hear her at all.

She was thankful when she could dismiss them for recess. She was worn out. Her hands shook. She was almost ready to quit right now. She did not want to wait even till noon.

Clara was so unhappy she hadn't heard the noise in the yard. Suddenly she realized it wasn't the right kind of noise.

She looked through the window and saw that the big boys were throwing the little boys down and rolling them over the ground with their feet, on pebbles, rough ground, stones, and mud.

She was so angry that she forgot her own troubles. She left the schoolroom in a hurry.

A SMART YOUNG TEACHER

Clara Barton couldn't bear to see the strong hurt the weak. It always made her furious to see a child or animal mistreated.

She was furious now, but she didn't know how to stop these bullies. It would do no good to scold them. They would only laugh. It would do no good to threaten them with a whipping, for she didn't intend to whip anyone. She didn't approve of whipping.

Then she thought of a plan. It might work—she didn't know.

Fortunately David had given her his hunting-dog whistle that morning. It was so shrill and loud it could be heard a good half-mile. Clara reached the yelling rowdies.

She took the whistle from her pocket and blew a blast that stopped them in their tracks. This was something new. They were surprised. They wondered what she would do next. She surprised them again.

"I am going to give you a treat," she said to them pleasantly. "I intended to wait till noon. But it is so warm I think you will enjoy it more right now."

She pointed to the two largest boys, Pete and Bill. "Please go to the woodshed and get that keg of cider."

They went running. They were always ready for a treat. Clara then told two of the older girls to bring a basket of tin cups from the shed, and they went running. They also liked treats.

By this time the boys came with the keg and set it on the ground near the teacher. It had taken both of them to carry it, and they were puffing from the exertion.

"We will open the keg over there by the well," said Clara. "It's shady there and will make a good place for us to meet."

Then, to everyone's astonishment, she lifted the heavy keg to her shoulder and carried it with one arm across the yard to the well.

David was right. The bullies understood and admired strength. The keg of cider had changed their ideas about the new teacher. There were now respect and admiration for her on every one of their faces. The young rowdies even waited quietly for their turn to drink.

At last the treat was over but the smart young teacher had another trick to play. She sent the girls and younger boys back to the schoolroom. Then she thanked the older boys for helping her.

"You have been very kind," she said. "I want to shake your hands."

Poor innocent bullies! They didn't know what they were about to get. They soon found out, and they were amazed.

She grasped each hand and held it like a steel trap. Her grasp was so painful that they were glad when she let go.

Clara had no more trouble that day. There was no more impudence of any kind.

She knew the good behavior would not last unless she made it last. The coughing, shuffling, or mumbling could start again at any time. It was her job to make these boys behave.

The next day she taught the older boys a new game. It was a difficult game that required a great deal of skill. A ball had to be thrown and caught while the boy was running fast. The teacher showed them how to do this, and all of them were astonished at her speed and skill.

By the end of the week she had organized yard games. There was no more running wild all over the schoolyard. The girls played a game in one corner. The younger boys played their games in another corner. The older boys played in the center. Each group stayed in the space that was allotted to them.

Another thing happened that pleased Clara. The rowdies had been slovenly and had come to school with dirty faces and hands.

One day Pete came to school clean as a whistle. His clothing was clean. He looked as if he had just had a bath. Even his hair had been washed. The following day Bill came clean as another whistle. The other boys cleaned up one by one. In a short time there wasn't a slovenly pupil in the whole school.

At the end of the second month there were no more rowdies or bullies. There were just boys anxious to learn.

Clara Barton's first school was a grand success. All the Bartons were proud of her.

The Runaway Slave

WINTER HAD COME and Clara's first school was still a success. Every one of her pupils loved her and tried to please her.

One night there was a heavy snowstorm. David had Clara drive his small sleigh to school the next morning. He had tucked a bearskin around her and had put warm bricks under her feet. She wore an extra woolen shaw because it was so cold. She found she needed it while she was unhitching her horse in the school barn.

She brought wood from the woodshed. This shed was only a lean-to built against the house. Soon she had a big fire blazing in the fireplace. In the hot ashes she put bricks to get warm before the children came. Her pupils would put the hot bricks under their feet to keep warm in the cold room. Soon the heat had melted the frost from the windowpanes.

Clara started across the room to wipe the moisture from the glass. Just as she reached the window a face appeared—the face of a Negro.

At first she was frightened. Runaway slaves were the only Negroes in this part of Massachusetts. But they were never seen during the day. They left their hiding places only at night.

Kind white people hid them, fed them, and took them to their next hiding place. Other people could not know where the slaves were hidden. If their masters found out, they could seize their slaves and take them back to the plantation.

Clara thought of these things as she looked at the face in the window. It was a frightened face. The dark eyes pleaded for help.

She was sure that this man was a runaway. She needn't be afraid. She must help him. She tried to open the window but it was frozen tight. She talked through it. "Go to the door. I'll let you in and help you."

HIDING THE SLAVE

The Negro came in. The poor man was shaking with cold, but he didn't take one step toward the fire until Clara motioned to a stool by the hearth. He held his hands to the flame.

She hung her apron over the small window, for there might be persons in the village who would send word to this slave's master.

As soon as the Negro was warm he told his story to the teacher.

He had run away from his master. Kind white folks had helped him all the way here. He had been brought to the old mill near the school the previous night. He had been told to wait until a white farmer came for him.

He waited all night, but no one came. He was nearly frozen by morning. He had to get to a fire or die.

"Did you meet anyone on the way here?"

"No, missus, no one saw me. I covered my face with my scarf. My cap covered my hair."

Clara made him eat her lunch. She said that she would eat at a neighbor's. She told him he could hide in the woodshed all day. It wouldn't be cold in there.

"I'll try to find that farmer who didn't come last night," she said.

"Maybe he was scared to come missus."

"It's more likely he had an accident. All the roads were icy last night."

The poor slave looked anxious again, and Clara quickly reassured him.

"If I can't find that farmer, my father will take care of you. You won't be the first slave he has hidden on his farm."

"God bless you, missus! God bless your good father for helping us."

"The worst trouble will be keeping the children out of the shed," Clara said. "The older boys bring the wood from there to keep the fire going several times a day."

The Negro jumped to his feet. "I'll bring the wood right now."

Soon he had enough wood on the hearth to last until noon.

Then Clara told him to take hot bricks to the shed. She gave him the bearskin and the extra shawl. She cautioned him to be very quiet and then she closed the door of the shed. Presently a few pupils came.

Although they were half frozen, the children at once noticed the apron at the window. Clara had forgotten it.

"It will help to keep out the cold air," she explained quickly.

The boys couldn't understand why she had carried in so much wood.

"I thought you would be too cold, boys, and I had plenty of time," she told them.

SAM AND THE SLAVE

Clara dreaded to begin school. The room would be so quiet that any sound in the woodshed would be heard. What if the slave went to sleep and snored? What if he sneezed or coughed?

By this time the pupils were warm. Clara had to begin classes, even though only a few children were present. She called a reading class to the front of the room.

Just then latecomers arrived. She had to send the readers back to their seats while she cared for these other children. Their wet shoes and clothing had to be dried at the fire. The children themselves had to be kept away from flames. Some of them always got too close.

Clara was glad to have the confusion and noise. Then a sound in the shed wouldn't be heard. However, her troubles weren't over. It seemed that all the children wanted to go to the woodshed. Boys wanted to leave their sleds there. Girls wanted to take cough sirup and comb their wet hair. She told them the shed was too cold.

She said they would have to use the back part of the schoolroom where their wraps hung. They obeyed her, but she was still afraid that someone would slip out there without asking.

The wood was being used up fast. Some of the boys wanted to bring in more right away. Clara thought they could wait until recess.

At ten o'clock Pete Bailey arrived, cold and covered with snow . He said he had had all the morning work to do—milking, feeding the cattle, and everything. His father had fallen the night before and sprained his ankle.

"It happened just after dark when he was hitching the horse up to the wagon," Pete explained. "He had to go somewhere to see a man."

"Ah!" thought Clara. "It was Mr. Bailey who was to meet the slave. He was the farmer."

Pete changed the subject quickly. His dog had followed him to school, he said. Could he bring him in out of the cold? Sam would be quiet. He would lie by the fire and sleep all morning.

Miss Barton consented, and Sam was called in. The dog wouldn't lie down by the fire, though. He ran about the room, sniffing as if on a scent. Then he stopped at the shed door. He sniffed and barked sharply. Pete and Clara tried to drive him away, but he wouldn't leave.

"There is some animal in there," declared Pete, "a squirrel or chipmunk or something. I'll let Sam in, Miss Barton. He'll get it."

"No! no! We musn't allow it to be killed. It came to us for help—to get out of the storm."

This was reason enough for the children, but it didn't stop Sam. He jumped at the shed door and barked excitedly.

Clara knew he had heard a noise in the shed. Something had to be done at once, and the clever Miss Barton did it.

CLARA'S KINDNESS

"Children," said the teacher, "I am afraid you will have trouble getting home this afternoon. It may snow all day and there may be very heavy drifts. Besides, it is impossible to keep this room warm. School is dismissed for the day. I will let you go now."

She asked Pete to stay a few minutes to help her. She didn't really need him, but she had to find out about his father. The Negro had to be taken somewhere.

When the other pupils had gone they put ashes on the fire. They took the wood away from the hearth and moved the stools back from the fireplace. Clara checked to see that her desk was in good order.

Pete was ready to get the sleigh. Clara could not put it off any longer. She must ask him now. "Pete, did you ever hear about the white men who help runaway slaves?"

The boy's face turned red. He didn't answer. He turned his head. She couldn't see his face.

"You needn't be afraid, Pete. I am hiding a slave in the woodshed now."

"Oh, Miss Barton! Why, I didn't think—I supposed it was some animal. No wonder you didn't let Sam go into the shed."

"He came here to get warm. He waited in the mill for someone all night. He didn't know the man's name."

"It was my father. I went to the mill this morning, but the Negro wasn't there."

"Was your dog with you?"

"Yes, and he got the man's scent. That's the reason he is barking. He wants me to know. He helps us with the slaves. He guards them sometimes. He wouldn't hurt one of them."

"Anyway, you had better hold him while I open the door. He might spring."

Pete was right. Sam calmed down as soon as the Negro came out. He followed the man to the fire. He sat close to him and licked his hand.

The man was pleased. "Sam helps a poor slave too," he said. He patted the dog's head.

Pete brought the sleigh. The Negro covered his face with his scarf and his hair with his cap. Miss Barton made him use the extra shawl.

174

Anyone who was passing by as they left would think the teacher was taking one of the big boys home. Everyone who lived in and around Texas Village knew that Miss Barton always went out of her way to help her pupils. That was one of the reasons they liked her so well.

Of course she would make the boy take her extra shawl. That's the kind of person she was.

The Most Famous Woman in America

ONE NIGHT IN 1867 a large hall in Washington, D. C., was crowded with people. The greatest of American war nurses was to speak—Miss Clara Barton.

She had nursed sick and wounded soldiers in the Civil War of 1861-1865. She had been right up at the front, too! She was always in danger. Sometimes she was under enemy fire.

Miss Barton was now the most famous woman in America. She had done the greatest thing for wounded soldiers that had ever been done by anyone in the United States.

She had found the way to save lives.

She hadn't liked the way the army took care of the wounded. She said their hospitals were splendid but too far from the battlefields. Many men died on the way before they received treatment. Miss Barton said they should be treated at the front, as soon as they could be carried off the field·

Her plan had been adopted. Aid stations were now set up near every battlefield. Thousands of soldiers had been saved by them.

Their families were grateful to Miss Barton. The whole nation was grateful. People loved the sound of her name.

Tonight a group of young nurses was in a box to the left of the stage.

"Just imagine!" exclaimed one. "Clara Barton was the first woman nurse to go to the battlefield—the very first in America."

"She had a hard time getting permission," said another. "General after general refused. They said it was no place for a woman."

"But that didn't stop Clara," said the third, smiling. "She went to other generals, army doctors, chaplains, quartermasters, colonels, and captains.

"She went to everyone she knew and everyone her friends knew. Finally she succeeded. She obtained permission to join the Army of the Potomac in 1862."

"Hurrah!" cried one, and all the white caps nodded.

"How could she do all that?" asked a new nurse. "I thought she was timid."

The nurse from Massachusetts answered. "She was. She still is. Her relatives say that she dreads these lectures."

"Why is she speaking, then?"

"To get more help for sick and wounded soldiers. She is devoting all her time and energy to this. She has spoken in all the large cities in the East, and she is still lecturing to large crowds."

The new nurse shook her head. "How can she be a good speaker if she is so bashful?"

"Her relatives say she forgets herself when she begins to talk about the needs of soldiers. She becomes another person, with the courage to face any audience anywhere. Just wait. You'll see what I mean. You'll love her."

"I love her anyway," said the new nurse. "I think she is wonderful."

Again white caps nodded in agreement. They all thought Clara Barton was wonderful.

In the next box was a group of young soldiers. All carried canes or crutches.

"I am glad I'll get to see Nurse Barton again," said one. "She saved my life in the battle of Cedar Mountain."

"She saved me, too," said another. "I had been wounded for a long time. The orderlies wouldn't have found me if it hadn't been for her lanterns. She brought them in her supply wagon."

"They wouldn't have found a good many of us," said the third. "There weren't any candles or any lanterns in our camp. Our supply wagons hadn't come up."

"I don't see how Nurse Barton could get her wagon up to the front with her supplies," said the fourth.

"There's a lot of difference between a single four-mule wagon and a train of 'em, four or five miles long."

"That's true, Lucien. Anyway, an angel from heaven couldn't have been more welcome. We were starving, and she brought food."

"Do you remember the cornhusks our doctors were using for bandages?" asked Will. "Then do you remember the rolls of soft white bandages that Miss Barton brought?"

The others nodded and smiled.

"She was a real manager," said Joe. "In about three minutes she had things moving."

"She had fires made, kettles swung, water boiling, and food unpacked in no time at all," said another soldier.

"And she herself was making gruel," said Lucien. "Talk about angels from heaven!"

"In more ways than you can count," added James. "She wanted to live the way we boys lived. She didn't want comforts we couldn't have."

"That's a fact," agreed Joe. "I know she refused a carpet someone offered for her tent. She said soldiers were sleeping on the ground."

"She wouldn't take anything but a soldier's pay," said Robert. "She told me that herself."

"If she said it, it's true," declared Lucien.

The others nodded gravely.

Across the hall in a box to the right, there were four army doctors and surgeons who knew her well. All of them had worked with Nurse Barton at the front.

"She was the bravest woman I ever saw," said one. "She helped me operate all night long, by candlelight, too."

"She helped me at the battle of Antietam," said another. "We were so close to the front that our faces were black with the smoke of powder."

"She waded in the mud at Falmouth," said the third. "She was helping the orderlies look for wounded men."

"Clara Barton never ran away from anything she thought was her duty," declared the fourth.

"No! Never!" agreed the others.

In an adjoining box were four army officers. Miss Barton had worked in their camps. All of them knew her well.

"I have often thought of her narrow escapes," said a general. "She was often under enemy fire. Once her skirt was riddled with bullets when she was crossing a bridge that was being shelled. She never seemed to be afraid."

"And such a bridge!" exclaimed a major. "It was just small boats close together and rocking with the strong current. It's a wonder she didn't fall into the river."

The captain smiled. "She told me afterward she had practiced for this when she was a girl. She learned to cross a river on teetering logs."

"It was a good thing she learned to ride horseback when she was young," said a colonel. "One day we had to ride at breakneck speed to escape from the enemy. She kept up with us."

"It looks as if she had been getting ready for this war all her life," said the general. "She was an athlete from the time she was thirteen."

"That's the reason she was able to stand the hardships of war," said the colonel. "A weaker woman wouldn't have lasted one day."

Now all talking stopped, for the meeting began. The Reverend William Fisher came on the stage.

184

He had charge of the meeting. He was followed by a lady. She was small, and she had dark eyes and hair. Her face was pleasant and kind.

The instant she appeared there was a thunder of applause. The large audience rose to its feet and a thousand voices called, "Miss Barton! Miss Barton!"

The little lady bowed, smiled, and waved her hand. The applause went on and on. Miss Barton waved again and again.

At last the people were quiet and she began to speak. She told something about her work as a nurse in the army camps. But she talked more about the needs of soldiers who were still in hospitals.

When she finished there was long applause.

Then again the audience rose and stood until she had left the stage.

They couldn't do enough to show how much they loved and respected her.

Fifteen years later, in 1882, another great crowd of people was in this same hall in Washington, D. C., to hear Miss Clara Barton speak.

Again she was the most famous woman in the United States. Again she had started something that had never been done before by anyone, man or woman, in this country.

She had founded the Red Cross in America.

Everyone in the crowded hall was talking about this. They all knew that Miss Barton had worked for years to get this country to join the International Red Cross. It had been established in Europe twenty years before. But America had been slow to join. Many officials didn't see the need for a Red Cross chapter here.

"We won't have another war in this country," they said. "It is impossible."

Miss Barton didn't agree with them. She remembered the Civil War too well.

"There will be other wars," she said, "and we must be ready to take better care of the soldiers who are wounded."

She went to the White House to talk with President Hayes about the Red Cross.

Later on she went to see President Garfield. Still later she talked with President Arthur.

She talked with senators and representatives. She made public speeches in all parts of the country.

At last, under President Arthur, the United States signed the treaty with sixteen other countries. Now our country was a member of the International Red Cross.

This new chapter, The American Red Cross, had made Miss Barton its first president. The meeting tonight was in her honor.

Now the officers of the Red Cross were coming onto the stage and people began to applaud the woman who was responsible for this treaty.

There was no need to tell the audience which person on the stage was Miss Barton. They had seen her picture many times in the newspapers recently. Her hair was gray now, but her dark eyes were as bright as ever. She was still small and slender.

There was a thunder of applause when the people saw her. Everyone stood, and hundreds of voices cheered her.

The gray-haired lady bowed and smiled and waved her hand. Again and again she tried to speak, but the applause went on and on.

At last there was quiet and she began to speak to them. Everyone listened intently.

She said this Red Cross treaty among nations was a great and noble deed. Her heart was singing with happiness because her own country had now put its seal on the treaty. She told them that the Red Cross could serve in time of peace as well as during a war.

There were only a few Red Cross rules, she explained. The most important was that all men who were wounded in war would be cared for. It did not matter whether they were friends or enemies, black, white, yellow, or red.

The next most important rule was that no Red Cross workers, doctors, or nurses would be captured or put in prison by the enemy.

"The American chapter has now added one more rule for the United States," Miss Barton said. "It will help whenever there is a fire, flood, cyclone, hurricane, earthquake, or other disaster where it can be of use.

"It will go also wherever there is an epidemic, such as yellow fever, typhus, or smallpox, either in this country or in another country.

"It will be ready to serve whenever it can relieve human suffering. The homeless and the sick will be given shelter, medicine, food, and clothing regardless of their ability to pay.

190

"All of this aid will be free. Not one sufferer will be asked to pay a penny.

"The money for all this will be given by those who are able to help. The fortunate will aid the unfortunate.

"When there is peace we will train volunteer workers who can care for the wounded in time of war. We will prepare medical supplies to be ready when they are needed. Will you help us?"

"Yes! Yes!" shouted many people.

"We will have trained people ready to go immediately to a place where there is a flood, a fire, a tornado, or any other disaster. We will provide food and temporary shelter for all those unfortunate men, women, and children who are left homeless and hungry. We will have supplies ready to help those who are hurt or sick. We will give immediate help where there is an epidemic. Will you help us?"

"Yes! Yes!" shouted the people.

"I myself am serving without pay and so are these officers. Our only thought is to make the American Red Cross a success. Will you help us?"

"Yes! Yes!" cried the great audience. Then they stood again and applauded until Miss Barton left the stage.

"There has never been anyone like her in this world," said an old man.

"Never! Never!" said all who heard.